Mom's Metal Men

By

Robin L. Amrine

This book is a work of fiction. Places, events, and situations in this story are purely fictional. Any resemblance to actual persons, living or dead, is coincidental.

ISBN: 1-4107-4721-2 (e-book)
ISBN: 1-4107-4720-4 (Paperback)

Library of Congress Control Number: 2003092673

This book is printed on acid free paper.

Printed in the United States of America
Bloomington, IN

1stBooks - rev. 04/28/03

To My Girls,

Love Dad- (Pa'Pa)

Intro

A quiet place was needed for them now- after a war that had destroyed their home on Thelona; the most advanced planet in the Orion star system.

Safe, at least for the time, they would be able to raise their son without the fear of being hunted. Even though their son Kamarin, was an alien to the mining colony of L-2, it would provide an undisturbed environment that would allow his parents to teach him of his heritage.

His mother, would read to him each night from a book of which had no title; wonderful stories of far away places.

She had taught him also to dream. This was an advantage the people of L-2 had long since forgotten. Often she would say-

"It is the way, in which the creator sometimes talks to us- so be quiet and listen!

Her son grew, and was heavily influenced by her stories. Because he was different, his friends had labeled him as eccentric. He had no idea that he was being prepared for a life beyond what any young mind could ever imagine. For the stories his mother would tell him were not just bedtime stories, but were those of actual events- his parents once lived- in another world far...far...away.

And now, with his father's death, he was to inherit the weight of Orion's troubles, but he was not to face them alone...

"One"

In a mining colony on a planet called L-2, deep inside the Orion star system, some colonists, (men dressed in their torn work cloths, the women in simple white dresses), were bringing gifts to a little clay hut and placing them in the window.

"Why did he die?" asked a young woman- standing in a small crowd forming in the small clearing outside the little hut and clutching some flowers to her chest. She had just picked them for the deceased man- as the miners gathered.

"No one knows!" said one of the old men- worn out from the years of hard labor.

"He was busy talking with one of the elders, trying to tell him something, when he just collapsed." Another spoke up in the group.

"What will happen to us now? Who will take his place?" asked the young woman.

There was silence…

Then the door to the little hut opened and a beautiful woman appeared. She wore a long diamond spun dress, woven thinly enough to allow the outline of her body to be seen. It was worn only, by the widow of a highly ranked colonist, as a statement to all that her husband did not die concealing anything.

Standing before the crowd she spoke…

"I have heard your words of despair and I am confused. Why do you talk this way?"

The little old man stepped forward.

"Surely you must understand that we are now 'all' afraid of what they might do to us! Now that your husband is not here to protect us, who will?"

"You have nothing to fear!" The widow tried to assure them.

"Tell us then- what will you do when they come for you? We gave you sanctuary because your husband promised he would see to it that they were all destroyed, if they tried to attack us."

"I think your husband lied to us!" said another women in the crowd "Yes, he lied to us!" She insisted, when the crowd began to mumble between them.

The mumbling quickly raised to a chatter through the crowd.

"Maybe' we should tell the elders all about you and your husband!" yet another said.

"Wait! My son will protect us." the widow answered out of desperation.

"Your son is but a child of fifteen! How will he be able to stand against the 'great' armies of the Gorin?"

"I am disappointed in you…When we first came to your planet, we brought to you people many new technologies of our world. All of which you truly lacked, and now you question us? Where is your faith?" The widow Mithchel said while she nervously shook.

"We have little choice but to trust you!" Said one of the Elders, who had just arrived, dressed all in blue, and who also brought flowers to offer her- in her time of grief.

Turning to address the crowd, first appearing to have a humble nature, his mood changed quickly as he began to speak.

"Leave this poor woman and let her grieve in peace- now." the elder said in a sudden stern voice.

"But we are all afraid, Master." said the little man.

"Afraid of what? A woman, and her fifteen year old son? You people are afraid of your own shadows. This lady and her husband have been a blessing to our community. What would you have her do?" The elder was beginning to grow impatient with his people because Laith Mitchel, her husband, had been his friend.

"Yes what would you have us do- do you want us to leave?" said the widow, now feeling a little more comfortable with the elder by her side.

"Maybe!" someone blurted out after a short hesitation.

"And where would you suggest we go?" the Lady Mitchel asked.

"I have heard enough! Now, all of you leave this woman's home before I report you to the council as undesirables." said the elder.

The people left a little reluctantly of course, but they went on their way without further disruption. For the elders' act- would surely cause them to be banished from the colony.

"I'm very sorry my 'Lady' Mitchel, they have always been weak and you have known this."

"I have, but I so very much hoped that they would change. I am afraid we have only succeeded in losing their confidence."

"Tessa," the elder touched her hand, "they never had it to give. Again I am very sorry Madam Mitchel."

He bowed to her and after giving her the flowers- he departed leaving her alone.

She laid the fragrant bundle on a small table just inside the door to her home. It had often been her family's place to gather for meals and small talk.

She wanted to protect her son from what was being said outside. But it was obvious he had heard everything.

"What is wrong mother?" asked her young son Kamarin.

She made her way further into the dimly lit room.

"Nothing my son. But I think that it is time for you to know more than you've been allowed."

"What do you mean mother?" he asked.

She readied herself modestly for bed behind a curtain to her room. Then she went to him to tuck him in for the night. Something she hadn't done in a very long time.

Her eyes were filled with tears.

She could not tell her son why his father had died, and she could not tell him why he would never fit in with the other children on L-2.

She was torn inside because she was not yet in the position to say or do anything that might help him deal with the sudden loss of his father.

It was supposed to be- his 'day in the sun' soon. Soon he would be sixteen and a 'man', but he could not yet be ready-could he? He could not be old enough to understand, she thought as her son lay crying.

All that she could do was sing to him, like she use to when he was young, and wipe the tears from his face before they fell.

Her song softly ended as he drifted off to sleep. She ran her petite fingers through his hair, and then whispered.

"Soon my son, very soon. The time will come when you will have to know." She said and turned to go wiping her own tears away.

She stopped suddenly and reached to her shiny headband and took it off, along with her wristband that closely resembled it; both appearing to have been made from a strange metal; rich jewelry- for a poor wife of a miner. Clearly they were not made from any of the mining planet's resources.

She turned and put them by her son on his pillow. Peculiarly, she tells the pieces of adornment to keep her son safe, and that it was now 'his' turn to protect the people of Orion.

A few weeks had past and the Lady Mitchel and her son had gone on living on the mining planet L-2. Living always under scrutiny, for one reason or another, but for the most part, they were never harassed. Except now her son was being shunned, and it was on this day, her son was to celebrate his

5

becoming a man. Today was supposed to be his 'day in the sun'. But it was to be denied him.

Standing before the elders, Lady Mitchel found herself in defense of her son Kamarin.

"Why are you treating my son as you are? Don't you realize that the sun ceremony is very important to Kamarin?"

The elders of L-2 sat quietly as if they intended to ignore Lady Mitchel as she spoke on her son's behalf. They had hoped that by slighting her in this way, she would not feel welcome at the colony and she would leave, and take her son with her.

"Your son my dear lady- is a danger to us all, and our community must require that the two of you leave us."

Realizing that her verdict had already been given, she became outraged.

"Danger to whom? My son is the only one in danger. If he is found before he learns of…"

She stopped suddenly, knowing that she was about to give up her secret. She could not risk exposing her son- not yet.

Sensing that she was hiding something, the grand elder spoke.

"What do you mean to say- if your son is found? By whom?"

"Yes, are we in danger?" asked another who seemed to be the head elder, but must have felt too important to speak before.

"No! It is only that my son could be prosecuted for something my husband and I did a long time ago, that's all." She countered nervously, wanting to change the subject, but wasn't sure how.

She was sure to be challenged.

"And for what offense might that have been?" asked the head elder.

Suddenly one of the elders stood and asked, with 'great' concern.

"Are you in trouble with the Gorin?"

"No!" she said. 'God No', she thought to herself as she looked up to the ceiling.

"Then why have you been hiding out for all of these years here on L-2?"

"Yes, what better place for you to hide than under our most valued customers noses." asked another.

"Most valued customers to you- perhaps. But they are the most feared enemy to many others." Tessa added dutifully.

"Knowing we supplied the Gorin with the majority of their uridium to power their ships. How did you think you could hide from them here?" the head elder asked.

"You cannot stop something once it begins- it's too late!" she said. "They will come for us. And my only hope now, is that your pitiful lives will be spared- contrary to your belief of us. Only- there is nothing we can do now to stop it."

"Perhaps! But it may be that we can prevent them from finding you here. I am sorry Lady Mitchel, but we must ask that you leave our community."

Perturbed and sickened,

Tessa answers… "So let it be! On the next aligning of the 'great moons', we shall leave."

"No! I am afraid that it must be even earlier than that. It must be before the snows come," the elder said closing a large book of which the colonists believed had all of the answers for such things as these. Without it, they would have no excuse out of these sorts of situations.

Lady Mitchel knew that it was all theatrics however. Finally distraught, and feeling drained, she took leave of their secret meeting.

On the way home she tried to assemble some thoughts as to how she was going to tell Kamarin that he would not have his day in the sun, but in fact, they had been banished from their home. It felt to her to be a long walk, though in reality it was short.

As she entered her little hut, her son was waiting for her inside.

He was sitting in his father's chair and was engrossed in a book.

The room was illuminated by a 'sun- stone' burning brightly in the center.

When she sat down on one of the furry chairs across from Kamarin, made furry from the pelts from some of her husband's hunting trips, she immediately noticed his warmly lit smile. She knew he would be asking questions about her meeting with the elders, and she knew that she would be afraid to answer them.

The sunstone brightened to its first heating level. It was then that she was able to see what book it was that had captured her son's attention.

It was the record book of her and her husband's life before they had come to L-2, and before Kamarin was born.

She sat quietly waiting for the barrage of questions that were sure to come.

"Mother—these things in this book! These stories! They are about you and father?"

"Yes Kamarin, they are." She said as her expression changed to a look of loving concern.

"All of these wondrous things- were all real? The people, the places, Thelona, Mother—the WARS! All of them are real?"

"Your father and I could not tell you before Kamarin, not until you were old enough to understand. You were not yet old enough to defend yourself...let alone Orion."

"Orion? Mother, what are you talking about? I cannot change history. The Gorin are powerful and own everything, even you! Anyone who tries to stop them are food for their Toupins."

"You have not read the entire book yet have you? Well then, I can see this is going to be a long night isn't it?"

She reclined herself to a more comfortable position.

"Let me explain to you what that record book will be unable to reveal.

Your father and I were born, on a planet fourth from the great star Kallose. It was so bright and warm there. And our home planet "Thelona" had so much water that the land's plants flourished. I tell you Kamarin; you have not seen such colors. Thelona was a large planet, at least fifty thousand miles between poles. And although five billion people lived on our planet- none of us had any wants. Our technology was not built out of self-needs or greed but from the cries of our neighbors on Delta and Belladine. They were much smaller planets, with a lot less people. We had an abundance of food and other resources to share— and we did!

9

Robin L. Amrine

But it was not long until even less fortunate beings, farther out in the galaxy, found out about our generosity. They too asked us for our help.

So, we decided that we should send them each, one of our scientists to help improve their own resources. In this way we could help by sharing our 'technologies'.

But something went wrong.

All of these planets suddenly declared that it was no longer necessary for us to help them. Absolutely no explanations were given.

At this time we had no idea that one of our own people had turned against us and was teaching the inhabitants of Gore, how to create weapons. With these weapons, this scientist had promised them great strength and to someday rule the galaxy."

"Mother, they were the Gorin?" asked Kamarin.

"Yes! And the man was…"

"And the man was Voltar Ghans!" Kamarin excitedly finished her sentence.

"Yes he was," Lady Mitchel replied.

"But mother- how did Voltar get so powerful?"

"Voltar found that the Gorin were very warlike and it was not difficult to teach them how to make and use weapons. It took the Gorin only three years to manufacture their armada of attack ships.

When we learned that the Gorin had invaded our sister planet Skybieria, we knew we had to do something to stop them. We did not realize how strong they had become."

"What did your people do, mother?"

"They are your people too, my love!" She said with a grin. "We then consulted the memory man, and his great library of the ancients. With his help we were able to create the most formidable weapon of all. A Metal Man. A machine capable of taking on any shape it needed to confront its enemy and 'win'. They were made of such a strong material that they were – virtually indestructible.

"Where are they now?"

"It's not like we made an army of them you see. The metal men were very hard to manufacture since we were pressured for time. The Gorin, were to attack us at any moment, so we had to act. We were only able to complete five of them, but even with that number we should have won the war. But before we were able to use them, they were divided up and given to five Thelonans, and to them were given the title of the 'Guardians of Orion.''

The Lady Mitchel explained to Kamarin how the metal men were given to three men and two women who worked on the project and that she and his father were among those who were chosen.

Kamarin then noticed something.

His head, and 'wristbands' were beginning to tingle.

"Mother, you still have not answered my question. Where have the metal men gone?"

Lady Mitchel smiled as she watched Kamarin start to squirm a bit. And as she spoke her attention was now divided as her eyes were focusing on the figurine on his head.

"Three of the metal giants disappeared- along with the other guardians. Your father and I were able to escape and left Thelona during its final battle. I was pregnant, and your father had been wounded. We had

11

to leave our beloved home before we were found again."

"You were captured?"

"Yes."

"That is when you came here? Did the Gorin destroy your metal men?"

"My son, how do you think we came to L-2?"

Suddenly Kamarin's head and wrist- began to get hot, then hotter!

Looking down at the bracelet his mother gave him; he was astounded to see that it was now "glowing".

He looked to his mother for an answer.

With a gleam in her eye, she took him by the hand and led him to a table in the brightest part of the little hut.

"Take them off… Put them here." she told her son, pointing to the center of the small table.

Kamarin was always trusting and curious, and he did exactly as his mother wished and set them both on the table. His mother reached out and detached the slightly larger figure from its headband, and gave the band back to him.

"You needn't remove your headband. Do you see the light?"

In his mother's eyes he could see the reflected warm blue light which emanated from the two figures.

"Yes!"

"If you need them to help you with a menial task, just separate them from their bands. When you do, they will only grow to 'half' of a normal human in size. Something very convenient about them is that if they are needed for a life or death situation, they usually come on their own. Don't ask me how."

As if it knew that it was being summoned, its light became brighter. Kamarin was in awe!

From outside of the hut, the blue light could be seen through the thin fabric hung over its windows.

Kamarin's voice was clearly heard by two young men standing in the shadows.

Looking at the little metal man that quickly grew from the figure of his headband, Kamarin knelt down to look him in the eye.

He was stacked short, and his metal skin was polished to a mirror finish. Although small at this stage, he would have weighed at least five hundred pounds. That is if you were using a good mining scale. A small red pulsating beam of light stretched across his face above what should have been his nose. His hands were not really hands but were ball shaped. His fingers the same only smaller. The little man's arms, legs, neck, and even his torso had the resemblance of shock absorption units used on the heavy doors of L-2's ore movers.

Kamarin was beginning to get impatient and wanted to see him move- so he asked his mother...

"What do I do now to make him do something?"

"Ask!" she told him with a smile, sensing his excitement.

"But what is his name?" he realized he hadn't a way to address the metal man.

"You can call them anything you like my son. They now serve you, and will answer to what ever name you choose."

Thinking hard, trying quickly to come up with one, he blurts one out...

13

"Deke! Your name is Deke! Move two steps to your right and stop!" he said with a stern command.

As the little robot moved, Kamarin could see four, finger-like hinged toes appear from the bottom of his canister shaped foot. As he stepped down, the toes splayed out giving the metal man more support. When he lifted his foot, they almost disappeared up into his leg. Looking back where he had stepped, Kamarin could see that Deke had cracked the thick slated floor.

Lady Mitchel gave Kamarin a short grin.

"That is why we do not call on them in the house." she said getting up from the table. "It is late now Kamarin, and we should go to bed. So tell Deke good night."

"But mother what about this one?" he held up his bracelet. "Aren't you going to show me what he can do?"

"That would not be wise, because there is not enough room in this little hut."

As his mother retreated to her room for the night, Deke straightened to attention and suddenly reduced back to his 'adornment' disguise.

-*-

It was night now and most of the inhabitants of L-2 were asleep.

In the darkness, the young men lurking in the shadows, were planning to take matters into their own hands and get rid of Kamarin and his mother…

"Tomorrow you and Deet will persuade Kamarin to follow you to the valley, and there we will attack." said Ogel.

Ogel was a very jealous and vengeful boy, and always felt that he would have received more attention from his father if it had not been for Kamarin.

"But Ogel. What if your plan doesn't work and the elders find out?" said Ogel's friend Kotch, a skinny little runt who was afraid of nearly 'everything'.

"He's got to go! No one wants them here, I've heard everyone say so!"

"Yes, but the council gave them until the snows come." Kotch replied- carefully.

"No way! After tomorrow they will leave- I promise you." Ogel seemed to have lost all touch with reality.

Just then, from within the dark, another boy ran to join the spies.

"Ogel! I've told the others to be ready with their treaders, they said they would be."

"Good!" said Ogel. Facing the hut where Kamarin and his mother lived, he yelled, "Kamarin, tomorrow it will be 'your' day in the sun!"

The young men broke up their meeting to go to their homes leaving the dark shadows, unaware that something else had been hiding in the dark there with them.

The figure- a robotic probe, had been hovering just a few feet behind them all the while.

-*-

Kamarin was unable to sleep after his orientation to the first metal man and his curiosity was about to get the best of him.

"Let's see—the first thing he would have to do is to remove the figure from his wristband." He spoke quietly to himself. Now he should set it on the table…he thought. But this time- he definitely was not prepared for what was about to take place.

First, the table began to shake- then 'bounce! Kamarin's face lit up.

"What have I done?" he said out loud. He thought, because he had not listened to his mother he might have broken it. It was clear to him that "something" was about to happen- and sure enough it did.

The glow from the figure grew intense. It was almost so bright that he could not continue to look at it.

Suddenly, with a burst of power and speed, it launched from the table and into the four walls of the little hut. With no place for the transformation to take place, it found an open window and escaped out into the darkness.

Lady Mitchel heard the commotion and stepped out of her room.

"Well?" she asked, knowing full well what had just taken place.

Kamarin looked numb.

"Mother, I thought it would not hurt to call on the other, just to… I'm sorry mother but I think there is something wrong with him."

Kamarin tried looking for his metal man- partially hanging out of the window from which it flew.

"Don't worry, Kamarin. Once he finds that he was not needed for anything, he will return. Now it's time for bed."

_*_

The unwelcome figure hidden in the dark- hovered into the light.

Having observed the events that had just taken place, it started to blink with many lights. Humming and clicking, it sent a message back to its operator. A large Gorin ship positioned behind one of the small moons of L-2's neighboring planet Polaris.

"Something coming in over the low frequency band sir! Its being sent from our Delta VI probe on the far side of L-2." said a Gorin soldier- sitting at a very large computer console with many others, who also had an urgent function to perform.

Feeling he had not been heard, he repeated his announcement.

A small man perched on a pedestal chair in a wash of subdued green light and a bright one shining down in front of him, leaned forward into it.

His face- was revealed to be newly scarred from a battle not long ago. His eyes were opened wide- gleaming from the long awaited news.

When the soldier turned again to make sure that the 'little' man had received the report through all of the confusion in the control room, he noticed he had disappeared.

As the little man, dressed in black, ran down a long corridor, laser light beams formed a grid pattern across his chest. This served as a silent warning to the person on the other side of the big steel door, and that the little man had finally reached it. He 'was' expected.

As he tried catching his breath, he raised his fist to knock, but before he could he heard his invitation to enter.

"If you still can stand Voltar, you may come in." a low amplified voice came from a small external speaker above the door.

Voltar could hear the man start to chuckle, just before he released the button on the intercom.

"I am able thank you! And I will enter!" Voltar, the conceited "little" Thelonan, as compared to other human Thelonans, regained his composure and waited for the large door to open.

Voltar loathed having to answer to this new leader who had during the 'great-war' taken over in his absence. After all, Voltar was once a great scientist, one of whom his home planet Thelona had sent to Gore to help bring them out of a struggling poverty. But during the war with his people, Voltar had been injured and was not expected to live. Now he had returned and was determined to reclaim his proper place as leader of the Gorin people. The situation as it were, would never be acceptable to Voltar, and to his secret supporters.

Someday soon, he would again be ruler of the mightiest army in the galaxy.

"I realize you operate with a very limited capability," said Voltar, "but we have found them! Now what do you plan to do about it?"

"You believe yourself to be very witty, don't you? I really don't understand why you are on this wild bird chase, Voltar. Why do you let those two, trouble you so?"

"Because the power they possess could destroy us! But of course YOU cannot see that, am I right?"

"Whatever you say, Voltar." The Gorin leader said waving for him to leave and began laughing uncontrollably. He knew that Voltar wanted his leader ship's throne, but he was not afraid of anything he might do to try to regain it. He was leader of the Gorin now.

Voltar was furious and stomped out of their new leader's throne room.

As the door slammed shut behind him, he leaned back against the wall, clenching his fist and gritting his teeth.

"Someday you fool! Someday." Voltar struggled with his rage to conceal it, conceal it for a later date when it would do the most good.

-*-

"Where are you going, Kamarin?" his mother asked. She noticed he was leaving with his travel pack.

She had made it for him and she knew he only used it when he planned to stay out all day, usually hunting.

"Ogel invited me to go treading with him into the mountains today."

"More tunnels to explore?" she asked.

"Yes mother." He thought for a minute, "I'm just going to celebrate my own day in the sun." he lowered his head as he opened the door to leave.

"I am sorry Kamarin, they just don't understand." she tells him as she played with his hair that was falling in his eyes.

She still hadn't the heart to tell him yet that the council had ordered them to leave the colony.

"I love you mother. I will be back as soon as I can." He stopped for a moment. "Mother- have you ever thought of leaving?"

Shocked, she wondered if he knew.

"No- uhm, I hadn't, but- mm you never know. Why do you ask?"

"I have." was all that he said as he grabbed some smoked meat from the table and boltcd from the little hut to the dirt road leading out of town.

He has grown so fast, so soon, she thought, we 'will' leave- and we will celebrate his day. For his destiny is not to die in some mine. "I will tell him when he returns." She spoke boldly out loud nodding her head to reassure herself.

-*-

"Hey! Where is everyone?" Kamarin asked walking into the shed where Ogel usually kept his treader machine.

Stepping out from behind the only machine left was a young man named Kotch. Kamarin did not know him very well, only that he was a friend of Ogel. Strangely appearing very nervous, he answered...

"Oh, we're suppose to meet them at the crossing." He said nervously shaking his legs.

"Why didn't they wait?"

"Oh- you know Ogel, when he wants to do something, he just does it and no one better get in his way."

"But I thought I was going with him on his treader?" Kamarin asked, guardedly, still wondering why the plans were different this time out.

Trying to bait the trap, or at least keep the prize hooked, Kotch perked up and suggested…"We can use mine- there is more room for us both anyway!"

Kamarin agreed and as they walked to Kotch's machine, he tried to convince himself that this wasn't any different from any of their other excursions- but he could not. Ogel had never acted this way before. All the other times he had been so organized that there were never any mix-ups.

Kamarin climbed into the back seat of the treader. Kotch had already started the twin engines of the cat track machine.

The front of the machine was largest, supporting the two large motors powering the large track beneath it. Trailing behind the power cabin were progressively five smaller cubicles jointly attached serving as storage compartments. All were sitting on wide skis for desert travel.

As the fire breathed from the exhaust, the engine blew sand away from both sides, heavily dusting everything inside the shed.

Kamarin shielded his eyes from the sand.

With the tracks placed in gear, they sped away from the small collection of huts.

While the others waited for Kamarin to arrive, Ogel stood watching from a cliff where he could see the colony far away.

A trail of dust soon could be seen being made from Kotch's treader.

"Places!" Ogel yelled to the others, as everyone scrambled to their points of ambush.

For some odd reason, Kotch stopped his treader near the base of a cliff, one Kamarin was very familiar with. He and Ogel used to set up their fortified outposts there many times, fending off the pretended advancing Gorin; when they were much younger.

Kamarin stepped down from the machine to stretch after Kotch shut the engine down.

Kotch suddenly leaped off the track of the treader and ran to the nearby rocks.

Kamarin thought it strange- for him to take off running like that, well maybe he had to go?

But his answer was soon to come.

"Kamarin! Kamarin Mitchel!" Ogel screamed from the cover of the cliffs. "Today Kamarin, is your day in the sun! Too bad you will spend it alone out here in this forsaken place… Alone… alone and dying!"

"What?" was all Kamarin had a chance to say before a sudden rain of rocks were being thrown down from the cliffs above.

Several of them bounced off Kamarin's legs and his shoulders, and then hit him in the head.

"Why are you doing this?" he asked trying to see who his attackers were. He had never had his life threatened before.

He was on the ground rolling around to protect himself as best he could, but when he tried to get up, the stones just kept coming.

Then they finally stopped.

After the barrage of heavy stones, Kamarin tried to stand but he couldn't, because the blow to his head had made him dizzy.

He looked through his arms that were wrapped around his head and he could see that one of his assailants was now standing before him.

With one quick swoop of his arm, he knocked him from his feet and to the ground.

"Ogel!" said Kamarin "It's you! Have you gone completely mad? Are you trying to kill me?"

As Ogel got up, he presented to the fight a "Tonbouy", Kamarin had seen pictures and heard stories about them. They were knives used to kill woman and children in some Gorin raids.

"You're a traitor Ogel." Kamarin said, coming to the realization he would now have to defend his own life.

He carefully planned his next move.

"What does it matter to a dead man?"

Ogel lunged at Kamarin just missing his side. He raised the weapon over his head to strike again.

But this time Kamarin was ready for him and jumped onto a large rock behind him, kicking the knife from his hand. He then pounced on Ogel with a fury, smashing him in the face repeatedly.

Ogel tried fending off the blows but Kamarin was too fast, for the lower form of life Ogel had become. Suddenly, without warning, Kamarin was struck hard from behind and fell unconscious to the ground.

When he regained consciousness, he felt himself being dragged in gravel up a hill.

Not yet able to move, he could only wait to see where it was he was being taken.

Ogel, and his accomplices, had soon reached their destination with Kamarin in tow.

They had taken Kamarin to the top of a cliff that jutted out high over the great Granite River.

Finally waking enough to rise to his knees, Kamarin tried to pull himself up by holding on to Ogel's shirttail,

But he was very weak and was easily pushed to the ground again.

They all gathered around Kamarin like a pack of wild and hungry animals ready to devour their kill.

"Hey, what is that he's wearing?" asked Kotch.

Ogel quickly realized he hadn't noticed the figures Kamarin was wearing, he had never seen him wear them before.

And before Kamarin could stop him, he reached out and took the headband from him.

"What kind of talisman is this?" he asked.

"Give that back!" Kamarin reached out for it and Ogel kicked him in the face.

"Smash it, Ogel!" Kotch said as he began giggling uncontrollably.

Ogel threw the metal figure to the rocks and stepped down on it hard.

Frustrated to find he had not even scratched it, he pointed to Kotch. "Smash it, Kotch!" he said.

Kotch picked up a heavy stone above his head and laughed at Kamarin, now bleeding from his kick as he laid in the dirt. As if crazed Kotch slammed the stone down hard repeatedly, but still there was no damage to Kamarin's precious amulet.

Kamarin tried again for the metal figure. Clawing at the ground, he finally gave up as he watched Ogel kick the metal man over the edge of the cliff. Feeling defeated he stayed limp as he watched Ogel throw the other metal figure from his wristband over the side too.

Ogel turned to Kotch and was whispering something, when the earth suddenly shook followed by a low echoing "BOOM!"

"Argh!"

Ogel did a backward flip as the metal man rose above the cliff.

He was now monolith in size. All the young men could see was a huge arm slamming into the ground next to them as the hand searched for a hold. It was so large it could have easily smashed them.

The giant metal man did not look the same, but Kamarin could tell that it was Deke.

The young hoodlums ran down the graveled slope, leaving Kotch at the top frozen. If it had not been for the warm sensation he felt down his leg, he would not have snapped to run.

Standing now at the edge of the cliff, the metal man towered over Kamarin. And as Kamarin looked up at him, he saw that he was at least seventy feet tall.

When Ogel and the others climbed onto their treaders to escape. The metal-man reached down, to aid his master to his feet.

Kamarin pulled himself up and could only see the dust from their desert machines.

-*-

Back at home, Kamarin's mother stood in the doorway looking off into the distance. She waited for her son to return. Usually she had nothing to worry about. But she had an uneasy feeling she could not shake.

She watched as two strangers passed through the front gates of the colony, upon their arrival. Very few visitors ever came to the colony and she did not recognize them as being from a neighboring village.

The cold chill she got from the strangers made her step back- into her little hut.

Spying on them from the window, she saw the two men stop a young woman crossing the square.

As the woman talked, they appeared to scan the layout of the village. Apparently having asked their last question, the young lady pointed straight to her in the window.

Tessa ducked behind the curtain, and knew right away that they were Gorin spies.

Now she was very afraid. She began to gather up everything she felt they might need, putting them into three large cloth bags.

Suddenly, there was a sound at her door.

For a moment she froze.

With her ear pressed lightly against it she listened...

In a soft voice- she heard, "Mother- let me in."

"Kamarin! Thank the creator!"

Feeling a huge weight had been lifted- she quickly pulled open the door.

Kamarin was sitting on the ground with his back against the wall. Even though it was night, she could see the dried blood, torn shirt and the already closing wound above his eye inflicted by Ogel's kick to his face.

"Kamarin, are you all right?" she asked as she bent down to help him into the house. "What happened Kamarin?"

"I cannot believe it, mother. Ogel and the others have joined the Gorin. Mother…we have to leave the colony."

Realizing that it may already be too late for them, she returned to her packing. She stopped for a moment, to wet a piece of cloth in the drinking barrel and gave it to Kamarin to put it on his head. She frantically returned to her packing and was too busy to look at him.

Kamarin was surprised to see that she was already preparing to leave. "Mother, what's going on?"

"Oh, Kamarin!" She said and started to cry falling to her knees.

Kamarin ran to her. Hugging her tenderly. What is it mother, please?"

Trying to suppress her tears, she tried to explain…

"My son, at the meeting of the council, they ruled that you, and I- must leave."

"Then that is why Ogel and Kotch attacked me." Kamarin filled with rage.

"I am not sure. You see they gave us until the signs of the first snows. We had plenty of time to prepare to leave."

Kamarin was confused, there still had to be an answer to all of this madness, he thought.

"But there is something else." She definitely had his attention now. "When you were gone, two men came to the colony. I am not sure, but I think they could be here looking for your father and I."

"They are here now?"

Robin L. Amrine

"Yes."

"Then we must leave tonight!" Kamarin began to help his mother. "The Gorin will find us, won't they mother?"

"I don't know Kamarin- I just don't know."

-*-

At this time of year, the sun burned bright over L-2. Usually allowing the air to cool a bit. But today it was hot, too hot to continue to make the journey into the desert during the day.

Kamarin and his mother rested under shade much of the time as they decided they would need to travel after dark. Traveling at night would not be too difficult, their way, would be illuminated, by the many stars that burned bright in this part of the galaxy.

Kamarin knew the desert quite well, but he did not recognize the path his mother was taking. He was not aware that his mother was taking him to the very place where she and his father had first stayed having arrived on L-2, after they escaped from the Gorin.

She knew that they could stay there for as long as they needed and in reasonable safety for there was plenty of food and water. The best thing, virtually no one knew of the place. A little cave tucked away in the Boverstand foothills leading to the 'Jofani Mountains'- gateway to the cold northern part of the planet. She had long ago chose this place to finish teaching their son of his heritage and allow him to find his own destiny. Who would have known that destiny would have them return.

28

"Two"

Three years had past and Kamarin and his mother had survived fairly comfortable in their desert cave. But a different fragrance was in the air, and Lady Mitchel knew that things would soon change.

Her son was now a man and he was not brought into the world, only to take care of her. Her son's eyes revealed he was getting accustomed to living as they were- but it was not where he was needed. She found herself constantly preparing for the day that he would leave her, but she knew that his leaving would not be easy for her.

Still- he would have to leave her soon.

"Mother." Kamarin said, greeting her as he ducked quickly into the large mouth of their shallow cave holding his shirt in front of him, forming a basket.

"Oh good! You were able to find more eggs." she said gingerly taking them from him to put them away.

"Yes mother, but I will have to go out again to hunt for something larger to stock up our reserves before the snows come."

His voice, was deeper, more of a man's now, she never realized it before.

"Yes, it is getting colder at night. The snow will be here soon." she said as he was getting ready to leave again.

His mother walked to the cave's entrance, and looked over the edge and then stared into the night sky. Turning to face her son, he noticed a 'lonely' tear falling down her cheek. He had not seen his mother this way since the night they left the colony.

"Are you all right?" he asked her.

"Do— you have to go out again so soon? I mean its going to be dark soon and I was wondering if you would like to watch the stars with me tonight?"

It would not be dark for another few hours but he could see that she was troubled, and she often felt more secure after they took time out to watch the skies.

"Sure- I would like that mother."

Later when the sun had set and the fire was glowing, Kamarin set a blanket on the hill in front of the cave. His mother sat down by him offering a bowl of berries as they begin to gaze into the night sky, above L-2.

"Kamarin- do you see that group of planets over there?" she asked pointing over his shoulder.

"Is that home?"

"Well, it is as close as you can get to home, but it is only a few of the planets that were once neighbors of our beloved Thelona. You see the large green planet over there is Skyberia, our sister planet. Someday soon you will go there."

"As Guardian?" he asked, standing- stretching- as if he could somehow get a better look."But- I am Guardian mother! I am the Guardian of the desert of this great planet L-2. I am the caretaker of the ground my father was buried in. What could be more honorable than this?"

Lady Mitchel did not realize how hurt her son really was. She had prayed that the creator would heal his heart- through time.

"Kamarin, if you remember nothing of what I have taught you, please remember this! Whatever obstacles you may face, you will not overcome them when hate clouds your vision."

"But mother, they should be made accountable for the things they do!"

"Yes, but it is not you who will decide their punishment."

"Perhaps, you may be right, but I will have much to do with their fate."

Lady Mitchel could see the campfire's reflection in Kamarin's eyes as he stood before the stars of the night. However, the fire in them did not seem to be a burning hate. It seemed to cool with her son's love of life he had always shared with his father and her. Although he had kept his pain to himself, she somehow knew he would not be misled by it.

"I have to go out again in the morning mother- before the sun rises, so I'd better go to bed." He then kissed her on the cheek and excused himself.

"Be careful when you go, Kamarin. Remember there are some who still search for us." She stood wrapping the blanket around her shoulders, turning her attention back to the stars. Alone…she wept.

"We had a fine son Laith— you and I." She looked as if she were looking through all the stars. "Oh, how I miss you! I believe in him, my love. He has learned so much of the old ways. He is very strong too— Oh yes very strong! I am so tired my love…My love, we were chosen to be guardians…but Kamarin…our son…was born to be THE GUARDIAN OF ORION!"

-*-

Kamarin was a handsome young adult now. His long hair was a dark blond and his eyes were a green with a light starburst of brown. He stood at least a whole head taller than his father had and that again of his mother. However, his mother was not a small woman, and she herself stood as tall, as any of the doorways in the colony; from which they were banished.

He had grown naturally larger than the colonists-because they were originally from a close neighbor to L-2, the planet 'Daharee'. There they had to run down their own food and therefore had evolved a sleeker build. But Kamarin had grown quite muscular and had stayed lean- because of the many hunts that were necessary for their survival. Because of his cunning-prowess they ate well.

Kamarin was a dead eye with a 'bandgun'. A portable metal handle, "U" shaped at the top and joined together by a strap of latex. His ammunitions were Lungslugs, Landwheels and Ribstinger darts. He would not need the Landwheels today for the hunt because there would be nothing left to take home. Lungslugs were too messy too. So the most useful would be the Ribstingers.

While making his choice, he walked down a dried riverbed- preoccupied- he could only think of the far away worlds and what they might look like. He wondered about the Gorin and their ferret leader Voltar Ghans and what his enemy might have in store for him.

Suddenly a shadow appeared on the ground that completely engulfed him.

He looked up as a large winged bird, swooped down to attack. Raising his arm to defend himself, one of the huge talons of the giant bird- hit, raking across his chest. Kamarin was rolled over and over from the impact. He just laid there…

The bird turned again as it soared high in the sky.

Kamarin watched it with one eye in readiness as he clutched his stinger dart at his side.

The bird swooped down, closing the distance he needed to get a better shot.

Then giving the beast no advantage of a warning, he jumped to his feet- launching the dart.

When the dart found its mark in the bird's breast, the dart exploded and it fell to the ground, just a few feet from him.

With a little 'kick' to its head, he was satisfied, that the great bird was indeed now dead.

Kamarin then began the long process- to clean the feathers from its carcass.

After sectioning the meat, for him an experienced hunter took no time at all, it could now be put in his pack to carry home. He had inspected the large hole made by the singer dart it had done its job very effectively. The dart had used up its small canister of compressed air and had burst all of the bird's vitals.

After he finished tying the first chunks of meat together onto his pack, he slung it over his shoulders.

Then he suddenly remembered a story his mother had told him, of how the Gorin would train large birds to seek out and kill their enemy. The Gorin called them 'Tritons', a kind of 'Toupin'.

Feeling very uneasy about this large bird he had not seen before until now, he started for the cave with haste. Was the bird a Triton? He wondered, as he made his way back. Surely they had forgotten about us by now- he thought. But on the other hand why should they? Just the fact that they were still alive, would be reason enough for the Gorin to hunt them down. After all, he and his mother were as a knife being twisted eternally in Voltar's side. No, it will not be over- until it is over.

He looked to see if his mother was standing at the mouth of the cave- awaiting his return as she often did, but he did not see her. Screaming her name, Kamarin ran up the long slope leading to the cave's entrance. Once inside, he saw all of their possessions strewn on the cave floor. "Mother!" he yelled.

From the darkness he heard her soft voice cry out. "Kam…arin…"

He ran to the whispering voice- only to find her beaten and lying in her own blood in the middle of a white cave bear fur.

"Mother!" Kamarin could not hold back his tears. Holding her weak, fragile body, he knew that she was going to die.

34

"Kamarin, you have to fulfill your destiny. This...is mine. Please, my darling son, do not cry, you are so very good. Yes, your father would be so proud of you!"

"Mother, please- was it the Gorin that did this to you?"

"Yes." she said, trying to sit up but she couldn't. "You have to leave now."

"No, mother, I cannot leave you!"

"Kamarin, they will come back. They're looking for the metal men!"

"Mother, please- will you tell me- did the Gorin also take my father's life?"

"I am sorry Kamarin, but I could not tell you before because I did not want hate to consume you. And you were so young- so young. Yes Kamarin- they did."

"My hate- has turned only to sorrow mother," he said, hugging her.

Her pain was so great her speech began to slow.

"Your father and I were captured by the Gorin during the Great War. While they tortured me, they interrogated your father. He would not give in to them- so they gave him the drink of Despair."

"What is the drink of Despair, mother?"

"Voltar knew that your father could help him defeat the Thelonans and help him take over the galaxy. But he would never do that. That is when he gave your father the drink of Despair. It was a drink that contained a disease. After it touches the lips, you could die anytime after. But some would not die right away, only years later did it take affect. And then it would strike you down suddenly, the same as it did your father. And there was no known antidote."

Feeling the pain from the beating she received from the Gorin for not revealing where her son was, she winced closed her eyes and squeezed Kamarin's hand. "I love you my son, I will always be with you." Her life slowly drifted from her…And she was home.

"Mother!" Kamarin yelled to the skies.

-*-

Kamarin knelt down on his knees in front of his mother's grave. Only a few days had passed since her death. He had left the cave because of the threat of being discovered by the Gorin. Now it was time to say goodbye but he was still a little numb from her passing. How would he fight an enemy he had not even seen yet? He still was not sure he was the one. He felt a strong urge now to go to that part of the galaxy where his parents had once lived. And if he could help, then he would.

Without a word, but with a tear, Kamarin took a familiar book from his shirt and piled more stones on top of it and his mother's grave.

He then held his silence.

The sun was out and the sand where he knelt was hot. He was alone but his heart was full of company. Kamarin remembered his mother's loving smile. Her calming touch and always when it was needed most. It was time to leave her but he would take with him his memories of her.

What is this? A squeaky sound coming up from behind!

Kamarin stayed very still, acting as if he was still in meditation.

When the sound stopped, he jumped to the side to throw a stinger dart. Just before he released it from his fingers, he noticed that the sound was coming from a little treader- like machine in which a young woman was riding. He was barely able to divert his dart. It narrowly missed her as it slammed into a large rock formation behind her and exploded.

Just then a large bulging beast, with hair over its entire body, jumped out from behind some other rocks nearby the woman.

Kamarin readied himself another dart now in order to save her from the beast.

Cocking back his arm to fire, the young woman raised her hand and yelled to Kamarin.

"No!" she said. "He is with me!"

"And who are you?" Kamarin inquired, still poised.

Regaining her composure, she answered valiantly. "I am Erin Noble, daughter of Asha and Badine of Thelona, Elshire district number seven. The Bendar here," she said pointing to the huge beast, "is the last Hondo of the great Granite people who have raised me since I was young!"

"And you are now old?" Kamarin asked with a slight grin as he lowered his arm and stood upright.

"I am as old as you!" she said, pointing her nose in the air.

"What do you want?" Kamarin asked, feeling pressed for time, although he didn't know why.

"Lort and I have traveled far to find a man and woman. But it is obvious you are not whom I seek.

You see the people I am looking for are great legends of Orion!"

"Why do you look at me as if I am an infidel- of sorts?" Kamarin grumbled.

"What are those things you are wearing?" she asked, pointing to his head.

"They once belonged to my parents." Kamarin decided to cut the conversation short and started to leave, picking up his pack, throwing it over his shoulder.

"Wait, where are you going?" she asked.

He ignored her and started down a nearby trail.

"I have to leave!"

"Wait a minute! Are you from Thelona?"

He stopped abruptly and turned, feeling somewhat honored with her question.

"My parents were from Thelona."

"What were their names?" she asked, enthusiastically cautious.

"They were Laith and Tessa Mitchel, and I am their son, Kamarin."

She drove her machine up closer to get a good look at him. Slowly she maneuvered around him in her machine while he stood still for her.

"Yes, he must be! He must be!" she thought out loud. "Come Lort! Come and meet the son of the great Guardians of Orion!"

With her invitation the giant beast Lort, tromped over to get a closer look at the stranger. With a low and gruff voice, he addressed the young lady.

"He does not look like a great son!"

Kamarin, annoyed with the remark, tried to look down at himself and his clothes, then started to walk again.

"It does not matter, Lort. Please don't leave!" she cried out to Kamarin racing her machine to catch up with him. "Where are your parents now?"

He did not answer.

"Can we come with you? Are you going home?" she asked.

"What do you mean? My parents are both 'dead'. I do not have a home now."

Erin now had realized that the grave Kamarin was attending, was one of his parents. Kamarin heard her machine stop suddenly, and he looked back and could see that she was crying.

"Why are you crying?" he asked.

"There is no hope anymore! All are dying or are already dead. Everyone is being killed and I have no way now to help them." As her tears welled up again, she covered her eyes with her arm and her body began to jerk. "All is lost- the Gorin will kill us all!"

"The Gorin? What do you know about the Gorin?" Kamarin was at full attention now. As if he had been hit by a bolt of lightning.

"The Gorin have been attacking all of the settlements on the other side of L-2, they have killed almost everyone. A Gorin army attacked Lort's colony and destroyed 'all' but him. He is the last of his race. The last of the great Granite People. We must warn the others. Will you help me?" She sadly looked up at Kamarin.

"How do you know they are coming here?"

"Kamarin, it is rumored that they are looking for your parents" Erin struggled to control her crying. She did not want him to think she was weak.

"And with my parents gone now, they eventually will come for 'me'." he said as he rubbed his chin and checked the skies above for enemy aircraft. "But I will find them first!"

"What?"

"I said that I will find them first." he said and started again down the trail. He believed he knew now where he must go. Back to the colony and wait.

"But they will kill you!" Erin yelled.

Kamarin turned slightly, gave her a grin, and continued on.

Lort caught up with him quite easily, with his large strides. The Bendar then reached out his huge hand and grabbed Kamarin's shoulder and turned him around.

"Did you not hear the little one? She told you, you will die!"

"You, though large you are, will not stop me! Now let me go, I have a date with a tyrant!" Kamarin felt a bit threatened by the huge beast but chose not to show any of his strengths yet, as they might be used against him. If the Gorin, are looking for his parents, he was sure they would trace them to the colony. But it all could work to his advantage. The hunter never expects to be hunted. He thought.

"Why don't we let him go? He is too young and inexperienced to be of any help to us", Lort said, quickly losing interest.

"But you do not understand, Lort, with his parents now dead, he is our only hope! If there is to be a future for us all- it depends on him. We must go with him, if he will let us." Erin looked to Kamarin with beggar's eyes.

"If it is what you must do, then I suppose you may." Kamarin said picking up Lort's hand from his shoulder and started off again.

The two of them followed him down the trail as he made his way back to the colony. Even though he and his mother were banished from their home, he did not wish any harm to come to any of them. There were a lot of innocent people who lived there. Their only hope was to warn them all before the Gorin attacked. The colonists had no defenses and an enemy, such as the Gorin, would easily destroy them.

To reach the colony, it would take them several days, but with such urgency, Kamarin was positive he could make the trip even faster.

Kamarin troubled himself with many questions, like, who were these strangers really? They could be Gorin spies for all he knew. Even though the girl's story seemed to be authentic, they still might be setting a trap for him. He was sure to find out soon enough. Her gigantic friend was very threatening, but if what the girl Erin said was true about his clan being destroyed by the Gorin, he could serve as a powerful ally.

The trail was getting pretty rocky and Kamarin's feet were starting to get sore. Looking back at his new friends, he saw Erin being tossed about as her treader machine rumbled over the stones. She appeared even more tired than he was. They would need to make camp now to rest.

"This is where we will make camp for the night." Kamarin directed them to a small clearing next to the trail. "It will be dark soon and it will get cold, so make sure you will stay warm enough."

"How do you know this?" Erin asked.

"You forget he is some sort of god and his presence will save us all!" Lort said, rolling his big eyes.

"Stop it, Lort!" Erin said, as she was not amused.

"I know because winter comes soon. The large moon, Tippoe, has joined in alignment with the other moons Titwan and Sibu. This will make it very cold on this side of L-2 tonight. And I am not a GOD!" Kamarin said, staring back at Lort.

Kamarin reached into his backpack and pulled out a piece of plastic cloth and laid it on the ground.

"What are you doing with that?" asked Erin.

"I noticed you do not have any water with you."

"Well we were trying to find some, that is how we found you. But what does finding water have to do with that?" she said, pointing to the material.

"In the desert, if you cannot get to the water, you make the water come to you!"

Erin watched inquisitively as Kamarin piled four stones in a square pattern and then laid the film down on them. Then with another stone at each of the corners, he stretched the sheet out on top of the others. Then he placed one stone in the middle, on top of the sheet.

"Give me that cup over there," he said, pointing to a cup they had brought with them in their own small pack of provisions. Kamarin scooped out two handfuls of sand from beneath the center stone and placed the cup there.

"That looks strange. Now I suppose you have to say some sort of incantation to make the water appear." Lort said, making a circling gesture over it with his big finger, attached to a very large hand. He looked at Kamarin with one eye, wrenching his face in a kind of smile.

"It is called science!" he explained, because it was obvious they had never seen anything remotely similar. "In the morning we'll have good ole' H-2-O!"

"Let me guess water, right?" asked Lort.

"You got it!" said Kamarin.

"No kidding, how does it really work?" Erin asked.

"Evaporation!" Kamarin sensed Erin hadn't even an inkling- as to any of it. "He's a little guy about this high," he said showing his ankle with his hand above the ground, "and he knows if you are a good person or not. If you are, the little tike' will sneak out here tonight and he'll leave you some water in your cup while you sleep." Kamarin was having fun now at her expense.

"Really? She asked, with her head cocked to the side, looking at him and then Lort with the feeling she was being duped.

"He is not telling you the truth little one. He is just playing you for a fool!" Lort said a little angrily.

"OK, I was having a little fun. You have not heard of evaporation?" Kamarin tried to smooth out the situation not wanting to upset the Bendar anymore.

"No! And I am not amused with you teasing me in that way. And I know that Lort would not like it if you did it again. If you get the picture?" Erin said rather smugly.

Kamarin paused for a moment, looking at them both back and forth.

"Uh-Ok, here's how it works!" He continued, this time a little more cautiously, much to the pleasure of his new found friends. "All day the sun tries to draw up moisture from the ground to make more clouds, but with the plastic here I am going to capture it before that can happen. The water droplets will run down to the center stone and fall into the cup!"

"Isn't that wonderful Lort? He will make it rain into the cup!"

Lort just acknowledged her with a "humph!" and rubbed his big face.

"You know, my mother used to tell me that someday I would learn of the wonders of her world."

"You said that she was Thelonan?"

"Yes, I said that she was."

"Then why didn't she teach you these things?"

"She did not have the time. She died suddenly when I was still very young. You see, my mother was often very sick. My father was a member of the council of the Ten. He helped work on a way to destroy the Gorin when they had lived on Thelona before the war. My mother was not allowed to know of these science things because my father told her that she would be safer not knowing. My father did not tell her what the council was making but he gave her subtle hints. My mother would talk to the other wives and try to put the puzzle together. By the time the war had started, she believed she knew what it was that was so secret.

When the Gorin, were suppose to attack, mother said that five very special people were given the secret of Orion, they had been chosen by the high council.

Everyone had separated to counter attack the Gorin armies from many fronts but before they could be defeated, the Gorin took many prisoners. One of them was my mother. The Gorin took them to work on an ice moon. Somehow they had found out about the Ten's secret creations and tortured my mother for more information. But she would not tell them to save herself.

When my father received word that the Gorin had taken my mother, he and two other Thelonans tried to save her, but they too were captured! The Gorin tortured my mother hideously.

She never told me what it was they wanted. She just told me that it would be safer for me not to know. Somehow they were able to escape and come here. My father died when I was very young and I did not know him. She told me it was a disease left over from the war that took him.

The terrible torture they put my mother through caused me to be born without legs and that is why I have to use this machine. It rages me when I think of it! You see, not only do I want to see them destroyed because it is only right, but I WANT REVENGE!" She gazed at Kamarin while she fought to hold back her tears.

"If you want me to help you get revenge, you have contacted the wrong person."

"Well, if you don't, then Lort will help me. He has a score to settle with them too, you know."

"Then you will die," Kamarin said, poking at the fire Lort had built as Erin shared her story.

"Is it your wish to disgrace your parents name?" she asked, as it became more difficult not to cry.

"It would be a disgrace if all that I sought was revenge. Revenge would only benefit you and be a small one for me but it would not help Orion to be free." he said as he got up to gather more wood. "How do you sleep in that thing?"

Her arms folded, she gazed at the flames. "I don't."

"Well, whatever you have to do, you might want to think about getting some sleep now." Kamarin said with his back to her picking up a small piece of wood.

"Three"

Morning came with the expected chill. A light blanket of frost covered the ground, and Erin and her friend Lort. Erin woke to find Kamarin was not on the blanket he had gone to sleep on in the night. Frost had covered it too. She looked around and over her shoulder, she saw Kamarin slumped over on the hill next to their camp with his back turned to them, then she realized he was watching something. She motioned to Lort, who was slowly waking, to help her into her treader machine.

Lort picked her up and sat her in the opening at the top of the cube-shaped machine.

She quickly adjusted herself, zipping up a skirt around her waist that now made her a part of the machine. Feeling for the control pads with her hip muscles in the socket which was her seat, she charged up the hill to see what Kamarin was looking at.

"What are you doing?" she asked, coming to a stop at his side.

"You're awake- good!" he said. "We may be too late."

"Why?"

"Last night I heard something in the sky pass over us but I could not see anything. But then I could see those lights over there. They must have flown right over us last night and didn't even see us."

"You can be thankful of that. I told you they're going to kill everyone didn't I?"

"Gather your things, you and Lort. We have a long way to go yet and we need to get started."

As Kamarin checked the contents of his pack, he stood waiting for the others to join him. He then looked down to his wrist and whispered, "I hope your ready?"

The metal figure glowed with a faint blue light and started to blink. Kamarin smiled and looked to the sky.

-*-

It was dark when they made their way to the back of the outer huts in the colony. It was very quiet, in fact, Kamarin knew that this was out of the ordinary. Often the colonists would be on the move at this time of day finishing up their daily chores.

Slipping around the huts and down the small dark walkways, keeping close to the shadows, the three slowly made their way to the clearing at the colony's center.

There in the courtyard were two of the elders kneeling beside each other, their hands bound behind their backs. They dared not move for behind them standing in a line, were at least ten Gorin soldiers!

"So that's what they look like!" Kamarin suddenly started for them wanting to help but Lort held him back.

Far out into the darkness, in front of the two hostages, came a figure into the light.

The soldiers in assembly stood abruptly at attention as a dark figured man was escorted to the two elders.

Then the rest of the colonists were ushered from their homes, by even more Gorin soldiers to be audience to their small but ruthless leader, Voltar.

"I am Voltar! Leader of the Gorin!" He dearly loved to hear his name pronounced in this way and jumped at the opportunity when it was presented. Even though he was not really their true leader, as of now, he was still able to boast because he trusted his soldier's allegiance and word of his tyranny would not reach Gore.

"You have among you two fugitives of the people of Gore, 'two' prisoners of war whom we mean to find and bring them back to face justice. They are not only criminals to us but they have committed unspeakable crimes to many others in the galaxy. They have lied to and murdered innocent people."

"That's a lie! They never..." Kamarin began to move again but Lort's grip just grew even tighter.

"Kamarin, stop! Those people know he's lying, he will say anything if it might benefit him. I am sure they can see through his deception." Erin was afraid he would draw unwanted attention to them- if he would not be quiet.

"If you do not bring these people I seek, we will be forced to destroy your village, and we will start with these two here. Now I require them to the delivered to me by sunrise. Their names are Laith and Tessa Mitchel."

"No! They can't do this." Kamarin said as he tried to leave again.

Erin looked to Lort and shook her head as Lort moved Kamarin up against a wall.

"Let me go, large one!" Kamarin insisted.

"Please, Kamarin wait until morning, it will give us some time."

"Does it really matter? One way or the other we will have to fight them to save these people," said Kamarin.

Erin was afraid to admit it but he was probably right. She just could not see how Kamarin thought he might be a match against the mighty 'Gorin'. She believed him to be mad or, that he was more than he appeared to be.

Kamarin led them down more dark alleys, until they reached a small hut at the edge of town. He knew that the colonists would have boarded up what used to be his home because they would feel uncomfortable using a hut whose previous occupants had been banished.

The place was dark, damp, and cold. Kamarin did not feel it was home any longer.

When he entered his parent's room, the only thing that had been left after the colonists ransacked the hut was his mother's shawl; laying in the middle of the floor. He picked it up and put it to his face taking in the fragrance that had permeated the soft fur. He remembered his mother as she carefully cleaned and treated the hide to feel so soft. Not wanting to leave a part of her there, he threw it over his shoulders.

The only room in the small hut with any light was coming from the hut next door. The sun had completely gone down now leaving the air cool.

Kamarin noticed that Erin had snuggled up to Lort's warm fur, in the corner as she prepared to sleep. He crept to the window facing the courtyard when he caught his foot on something. Looking down, he saw the cracked slate in the floor where Deke had stepped long ago. He let his mind drift for a moment to reflect. It seemed as if it were only yesterday.

Kamarin could see that the elders were still being made to kneel in the cold, as an example to all others.

"They'll die out there," he said.

"Try to relax," Erin said yawning. "I mean, what are you going to do? They out number us ten to one. Kamarin- tell me, why were you and your mother living in the desert anyway?"

"They were afraid of us."

"What do you mean afraid?"

"They thought that we would bring trouble to the colony if we stayed. It was this very thing they hoped to avoid by sending us away. But the Gorin are a relentless and ruthless people." Kamarin bowed and shook his head.

"Are you sure it was not something else they feared, like maybe the unknown and maybe the strength your parents possessed?" she asked.

"They had no idea what we possessed."

"Well now, you are here—aghh! And now you can save them."

While Erin went to sleep in Lort's side, Kamarin went deep into thought. He wondered if all that his mother told him was true. Was he the one? Was he the one who would use the metal men to defeat the Gorin? The responsibility he was about to accept was phenomenal. And yet, he felt a very strong and compelling urge to help these people. He was sure of one thing and that was that he had to see an end to these tyrants of the galaxy.

He, for a moment, looked to Erin in hopes that she might have words of encouragement, but she was now fast asleep. Although fatigued, he himself would not be able to sleep, not tonight...

-*-

Morning would come soon now and Kamarin knew that they must ready themselves before it became light. He pulled from his back-pack an ammo belt and then covered the pack with his mother's shawl. The belt held five Landwheels, five Ribstinger darts and twelve Lungslugs. He slung the belt over his shoulders and then leaned down to wake his friends.

"Come on, get- up! Things are going to get a bit exciting pretty quick," he said, shaking them both.

Erin and her behemoth friend, Lort, woke suddenly. She looked as if she had seen a spirit-shaking slightly as she woke.

Lort stood picking Erin up with him and quickly sat her in her machine.

"It's not even light yet. What are you going to do?" Erin asked, rubbing her eyes while she zipped herself in.

"I don't know. I was kind of hoping that maybe you had an idea." he said.

"Me? Oh! Well I am honored but…"

"Listen! What is that?" Kamarin said, looking through the window, now without curtains. A loud humming noise was coming from outside the colony's courtyard. Kamarin bolted from the hut and took cover behind a tree at its edge.

"What's he doing?" Erin asked Lort pulling on his arm hairs, noticing Kamarin had suddenly left the little hut.

"Looks like he's trying to get himself killed."

Kamarin crouched at the base of the tree, peering through the legs of the people that had come to see where the strange noise was coming from. Something was there- coming down the dark street. The humming, vibrating sound grew slowly louder but still was not revealing its source.

Then it appeared- a long barrel of a strange gun was suddenly illuminated by the lights from the group of huts. The menacing machine of death hovered into the square by some sort of cushion of air and then lowered its barrel aiming at the two elders. They were frozen to their knees. It appeared to be a magnetic field that it rode on as the base of the machine swiveled.

A gunner exited from the armored shell of the machine jumped to the ground next to the Gorin leader. He wore a skin-tight suit made of a shimmery type of metal cloth so brilliant it seemed to give off its own light.

When this soldier took off his helmet, Kamarin heard the crowd gasp. But he could not see the man's face through the crowd, so he took the chance and stood upright and was stunned.

"Ogel!" Kamarin blurted out as the crowd opened up to look at him.

All attention was now on Kamarin as the people began to point giving him up to the Gorin.

A group of Gorin soldiers ascended upon him. He could not escape with as many colonists there to aid the enemy.

Struggling to free himself, he could see Erin charging her machine at high speed toward a column of soldiers trying to help. As Kamarin was forced to the ground, he could hear the crowd screaming as he heard Erin say-.

"Lort, no!"

It was Lort's turn as he swung his mighty hammer the way only a great Hondo of the Granite people could. Laying waste to all who dare to attack.

Before Erin could run over anymore Gorin soldiers, her machine was lassoe'd and she and the machine were tied to a tree.

Lort had no reason to give himself up as he smashed the soldiers easily with one blow. In fact, he was busy cleaning a path on his way to their leader. As the Gorin ran to him seemingly eager to give up their lives to him, he crushed their bony heads as they persisted.

Ogel did not know the giant Granite man or the young woman who was going nowhere fast tied to the tree. Her tracks whirled as they dug them-selves in. Ogel quickly surmised that she was Kamarin's friend. So with that, he jumped to Erin with his weapon drawn and pointed it to her head.

The other soldiers who were trying to keep Kamarin down followed suit.

Of course, Ogel knew it was time for him to put on a show for their leader. Holding Erin's mouth, he twists her head to him and yelled at the huge beast with dramatic results.

"Stop you beast from hell! Kill another and they too will loose their lives!"

Unfortunately for one of Voltar's men, Lort was still in mid swing when he heard Ogel's threat.

"OOPS!" Lort said with a grin as he regained control of his hammer and stopped short of Voltar.

Gorin soldiers poured over him and still could not pull him to the ground, but Lort did not resist now.

"Now I don't know you two," Ogel said, pointing at Erin and Lort, "but I do know you!" he said pointing to Kamarin, "It's been a long time old friend." Ogel strutted his stuff- before all the colonists and the evil Voltar; proving to them he now possessed the power over the situation. He also knew that Voltar would soon grow tired of his little show- if he failed to deliver.

Ogel was well aware of Voltar's stare now, as he was about to reveal Kamarin to him.

"Kamarin- KAMARIN MITCHEL! He went on gloating, "Where are your parents?"

Kamarin was outraged, trying to free himself and then he was thrown to the ground again.

This time the soldiers bound his hands behind him with steel cable. When they brought him to his feet again, he stood face to face with their leader, but Kamarin's brow had been cut in his struggle and he could not focus on the little man's face.

"So- you are the son of ones I seek?"

Kamarin remained silent. He wanted so much to see Voltar's face, to burn it into his memory. For the next time he laid eyes on him, he would make it the last!

"If you do not speak…then you will be killed along with your friends- plain and simple," Voltar said, standing on his toes to whisper into Kamarin's ear.

"Don't you think that I am aware of that by now?" said Kamarin through clenched teeth.

"Then you want to die?" asked Voltar as Ogel smiled.

"Hmm… no I don't think so." Kamarin said with a smile.

"Take this hilarious man away from me- NOW! And put them in the ship's hold."

The day was upon them now as the soldiers carried them off to one of the large Gorin transports. There they put them in its belly where they normally hauled raw ore from the mining colonies of L-2.

This part of the ship was almost round. Kamarin sat in the middle with a piece of cloth on his head.

Erin could see the door above them through which they were forced to enter. She was lucky not to have toppled over as she and her machine were shoved into the odd shaped room.

Lort was busy pounding on the sides, which were the floor. The noise was almost deafening. He had lost his hammer, but if he had it, he was sure he could break through the thin hull of their ship.

Kamarin yelled for him to quit.

After the echo had stopped, Erin moved closer to Kamarin so she could hear him speak. She leaned her head on his stomach and then looked into his eyes. Her tears began to come and Kamarin's heart melted.

"Please take me out of this contraption." she said softly.

He knelt down on one knee to help her. She leaned her face into his shoulder and squeezed his arm as he picked her up. When he stood with her, she did not move her head though her body trembled as she wept in his arms.

"Are you all right?" he asked, pulling her hair back revealing her innocent and pretty face. It was almost as if they were meeting for the first time.

"I'm afraid, but I'm also angry. Now it's all just hopeless!"

"What did you expect Erin? Please…be patient. Besides, the fun part is about to begin," he said helping her back to her machine. "You'd better zip yourself in."

"But Kamarin, do you think they're going to kill us?"

"NO. Not today."

"But what are we going to do?"

"For now…we wait." Kamarin said as he sat on the floor next to her.

Kamarin still had not been given the opportunity to see his captor's face and he was determined to before they made their escape. Oh yes, they could have made good their escape along time ago but there was the unfinished business to take care of first.

The large door above them opened and it was Voltar and his puppet Ogel. Kamarin looked away as if he were not interested.

"You!" Voltar said, pointing at Kamarin. "You are Thelonan? If this is true- where are your parents? I wish only to talk with them." Voltar said pretending to re-fit his black-gloved hand.

WORM! Kamarin thought as he turned to face his captor.

"So you only want to talk to them he?" Kamarin said calmly.

"Oh yes, of course, I am not here to harm anyone. No, no, no! Of course not. I only wish to gather some information that I am so dearly in need of…"

"Oh! Is that all? Then I will need to go and get them for you. But of course, I will need to be set free so I can go and look for them. Yes, I will need to be free so that I may bring them back here to answer all of your important questions. Yes, I will…"

As Kamarin went on, Ogel knew this was not like him and wondered for a minute if he had somehow suffered an injury to the head. Then he got Voltar's attention and shook his head to bring attention to the fact that Kamarin was acting only in jest.

Voltar was suddenly enraged and raised his fist in the air.

"You play games with me? Stop it! Stop this dribble!" he demanded.

"Oh yes, I am sorry! Somehow I forgot- they're dead. They both are you know, really they are," Kamarin said turning as if he was including his new friends in on the news. "You know, I really should have told you before, but you did not ask me, now did you? I mean you really could have given me the chance to tell you that they are both DEAD!" Kamarin said soberly and turned to look Voltar in the eye.

Stunned, Voltar looked back at Kamarin.

"I don't think this is a bit funny!" he said as he looked around to the others. "No, not in the least!" he turned to Kamarin again raising his voice. "Where are they?"

"Dead, you slithering Goatworm!" Kamarin wanted very much to have his hands around Voltar's neck.

Voltar suddenly regained his calm and his hard face broke out into a sick smile.

Kamarin saw fire when he saw how happy the news of his parent's death had made him.

"Yes, Voltar, but I am their son and you will pay for all that you've done- and for having taken their lives."

"Ah, but Kamarin Mitchel, by possessing you, I also possess the two. Soon I will have the others and as for you, I do not worry, for you will give them to me to save your friends. You will give them to me for your freedom or you will all die!" he said, and as he laughed, the door closed.

"It is not I who will die!" Kamarin said realizing Voltar could not hear him now. But why hadn't they tried to take the metal men from him? Maybe it was because Ogel had told Voltar about their power and their apparent loyalty to Kamarin that made them both afraid to even touch them. There really was no other explanation. After all, Voltar seemed to know an awful lot about them.

"How can you make a threat like that to him when we are trapped down here?" Lort asked Kamarin.

"People of little faith surround me!" Kamarin said as he walked to the center of the ship's cargo hold and sat Deke in the middle of the floor. "Now stand away- a little more please."

"Stand back- for what?" Lort asked.

"Look!" Erin said, "It is glowing."

"What is it?" Lort turned and watched in amazement as it pulsated.

The glow could now be seen in their eyes as it began to grow. The little metal man would not stay little for long as it was being summoned and it would soon accomplish that which Lort was not able to.

"It's growing!" said Erin.

"Yes, it is, isn't it?" Kamarin smiled.

As the metal man grew, it looked around and over its head as if it were sizing up the situation. Reaching out with first one hand then the other- Deke towered over them and braced himself with his arms up over his head.

The sounds of metal ripping metal could be heard throughout the ship as Deke began tearing at the ship's hull.

Carefully, Kamarin and Lort climb over the jagged edges of the torn ship's skin to escape but it was too far to jump to the ground.

"Deke!" Kamarin yelled, pointing to Erin for him to help her down safely.

Holding his hand out, Lort and Kamarin climbed on. Deke reached over and picked Erin up by her treader machine like a flower in a vase, then he lowered them all to the ground. The metal man then returned to finish what he had started- destroying the Gorin ship.

Smoke poured from the ship as its power plant was soon destroyed.

The three of them quickly made their way to the gathering of clay huts on the outer edge of the colony and out of danger.

Gorin soldiers started to jump to the ground to escape their burning ship.

The others, who had been left on the ground to imprison the colonists, began to use their feeble weaponry on the giant metal man's feet and legs. Deke's upper half was still inside their ship tearing out bulkheads.

In all the smoke and confusion, Kamarin waved to Erin to go to the street leading out of the colony. He then turned to see three soldiers making their way towards his friends. He ran and dove into the window of his at one time home and grabbed his back-pack. In the shuffle with the Gorin, he had lost his ammo belt and now he hadn't any weapons. Having little time to spare, he jumped back out into the street. Reaching into his pack, he grabbed a 'landwheel, and let it fly at the soldiers.

The explosive wheel made a sudden curve for the ground and met the enemy with lightening speed, leaving a flaming trail. As it hit the first Gorin soldier, it detonated, taking them all out at once.

When Kamarin joined the others, they suddenly heard a loud humming sound, coming from the top of the Gorin war ship and then it was gone.

Huge explosions came from the once mighty Gorin ship, which was now reduced to rubble and crumbling in a heap at the metal man's feet.

The Gorin soldiers kept up their sorry attempt to ward off the giant offender, but to no avail.

"You have to leave here now! Head north to the transport station and I'll catch up with you on the way." Kamarin directed Erin. Waving her on, he ran back towards the confusion.

"NO!" Erin cried out to him.

"Come now, little one!" Lort waved to her.

"But he could be killed fighting them alone."

"Take a good look, missy. Does it look like he is alone?" Lort pointed to the metal man.

As the explosions continued into the night, the light could be seen from miles away.

The bitterness of the cold came with nightfall.

Lort followed behind Erin as she guided her machine through the frost-covered desert at high speed. He repeatedly asked her to stop for he needed to give his feet a rest. His thousand pound girth was multiplied with every step.

But Erin could not control her excitement and was preoccupied. Her newly found determination to warn the others of the Gorin's coming and to leave L-2 was too much. She was so happy, now that she had found a leader who could defeat the Gorin. Her mother would have been proud of her. Everything seemed hopeless before she had found the Guardian. She knew the first time she saw Kamarin that he was something special.

Suddenly hearing a thump, Erin turned to see Lort sitting by the trail exhausted.

"Can we rest now?" Lort asked, his eyes revealed his weariness.

She hurried to his side and parked her machine close to him. "I'm so sorry, Lort." she said, giving him a big hug around his neck. "Just look at you- you look awful. Why is your hair turning color? It's white!" She began to run her fingers through it.

"It is the cold. It always turns this way when I travel to the snow country. For some reason it keeps me warmer."

"Truly a gift from the creator!" Erin said, snuggling a bit closer as she was beginning to feel the bite of cold now.

"I will build a fire for you, little one!" He said, standing up slowly, being careful not to knock her over as she clung to him.

She rubbed her arms trying to stay as warm as possible while Lort walked to a nearby tree and began to split it down the center with his bare hands. After braking the limbs, he laid the pile of lumber in the middle of the trail.

The fire slowly grew and Erin looked at him with a warm smile on her near frostbitten face.

"The sun is going down much faster now," she said.

"Yes- it definitely is going to be winter very soon. The sky has changed its color. It could even snow tonight. I will build us a shelter." Lort backed away slightly from the fire as not to become part of it.

"Lort."

"Yes, missy."

"I love you. You are my best friend of all." Erin said petting the fur on his arm.

"Why thank you, little one. I care very much for you too, for you are my family."

Taking the rest of the branches from the tree, Lort constructed a framework for a shelter and then grabbed handfuls of sod to lay onto the roof. The process took the gentle giant only minutes to do. They would sleep warm tonight.

-*-

There wasn't any wind just large flakes of snow. Snow and more snow.

L-2's moons shown brightly in the night, almost making the snow coming down a fluorescent color. Kamarin could not tell where the sky and the planet's surface met. In fact, he did not know if he was going uphill or down. He began to feel that he would never find his friends.

The cold was beginning to take its toll on him and he called out for Erin.

Then there was a shadow- or was it? His eyes began to trick him. He continually stumbled in the snow.

"I'm LOST!" he yelled, feeling beaten by the cold. Then suddenly his wristband began to glow, a bright blue.

He continued to drag himself through the snow. Every time he would stray from his course, the metal man grew dim. As long as he walked true, it would burn brightly, guiding him north to his friends.

"It's so cold!" he said, then suddenly a light blue haze surrounded him and the cold air that engulfed him became warm. So warm in fact, he soon was quite comfortable. He regained his strength quickly and kept on through the night.

"Lort! Wake up Lort. Wake up!" Erin said, shaking his arm. "Wake up I smell something."

Lort awoke to see Erin just inches from his face as he looked back at her cross-eyed.

"What is it?"

"Shhh! There's someone out there," she said nervously.

Lort backed up out of the shelter and found he was standing in at least a foot of snow.

Erin pulled herself into a better position to see outside. She could barely make out a figure looking through Lort's hairy legs.

"It's Kamarin!" Erin cried out. She hurriedly crawled to her machine and asked Lort, "Help me in!"

Lort obliged her as she quickly zipped herself in. "Kamarin! How did you find us?"

Kamarin turned and could not answer her directly he was too busy chewing on breakfast that he had been cooking for them all.

"Kamarin! Oh, how I'm so glad to see you." Erin said as she raced her machine over to give him a hug.

Kamarin dropped the little pan he was holding when she reached him, accidentally running over his toe with the track of her treader. In pain and teeth still clenched around his meat, he hurled upside down and backwards into the snow. Face down he let out a muffled scream.

Later, Kamarin and his friends were again on the trail north, leaving a lonely path in the white desert. It wasn't long before they discovered another small settlement. It had been totally destroyed.

In silence they slowly walked among the devastation. No bodies- and the buildings had been leveled.

Kamarin and Lort looked at one another in agreement, they were sure that it was the work of the Gorin. Had they destroyed everyone?

They had gone through several villages suffering from the same fate. But Kamarin was disturbed with this particular one as all of the buildings appeared to have been crushed. There were no fires and no sign of any laser blasts. If this was indeed the work of the Gorin, what sort of weapon had they used?

"Oh what a beautiful place," Erin said as they rounded the bend of the head-waters of an icy blue river and into a mountainous valley. Great spires of rock hundreds of feet high dotted the valley. Some looked as though they might fall over as they were large at the top and narrow at the base.

"This is the beginning of the Great Granite River. Isn't it a wondrous sight?" Lort said as they continued into the valley.

"Four"

Making their way through the forestation dotting the valley floor, Kamarin felt that they were being watched.

Then in a flash, a Gorin attack fighter swooped down around one of the huge rock pillars where they stood beneath. The Gorin pilot took aim and fired, blasting large chunks of granite from the pillar's face. Even though the three scrambled to avoid being hit by the laser blasts, they did not seem to be the Gorin's target. The blasts were aimed high above their heads, at the pillar itself. Not even the worst Gorin fighter pilot would have missed his mark that far off.

As he came around for another pass, the distance between them quickly closed. He suddenly pulled his craft upwards and fired again at the upper portion of the great rock formation. But this time, as if lightning had struck, his craft exploded above them in small pieces. It fell like burning rain.

"What was that?" Erin said, popping her head up above the foliage she had taken refuge in.

"A Gorin fighter!" Kamarin replied.

"What made it blow up like that?"

"I didn't see anything," Lort said, looking around on guard.

Kamarin motioned Erin and Lort to come closer, then pointed to a small ledge above them in the pillar of rock. From below where they stood, the tip of a large gun barrel could be seen sticking out.

"Why didn't they shoot us?" Erin asked in a whisper.

"Because one, they didn't see us, or two, they didn't want to. I am hoping on the latter," Kamarin said as he started stealthily around the rock's perimeter.

The others followed close behind.

Half way around with Lort bringing up the rear, he stopped suddenly with a puzzled look. Footsteps came up from behind him! When he turned quickly, he saw a little man carrying a large laser rifle so big he struggled to carry it. It was much too large for him. Following the three of them, he looked at Lort and smiled from ear to ear.

"Please, by all means continue, you are going in the right direction," the little stranger said.

Lort lunged swiftly, grabbing the weapon from the small intruder, but the little man did not let go and Lort happened to pick him up with it.

The little man kept holding on kicking and screaming.

"Let go of my laser, it's mine! I found it fair and square." The stranger said, swinging from Lort's arm.

With the sudden commotion, Kamarin and Erin were in readiness for an attack from all sides. Luckily it did not transpire.

"Who are you?" Lort asked, holding the gun higher to get a better look at him.

"Let go of…my…weapon. It's mine, mine, mine!" he said, wrapping his feet around the rifle. "Besides, it is none of your business who I am. Now, put me down! Put me down!"

"If you do not tell me, I will pinch off your head at your shoulders! Then you will have nothing more to care about," Lort said, swatting at the little man with his other hand as he tried to bite the one holding the gun barrel.

"OK, OK! I will answer, just let me down, let me down!"

Lort looked to Kamarin for his approval and with Erin training her weapon on the little man, Kamarin gave him the OK.

"Where did you find this behemoth, anyway?" the little man asked Kamarin.

Kamarin smiled remembering the first time he had see Lort. "Excuse me," said Kamarin. "Can't you see that we have a slight opposition to strangers sneaking up on us from behind?"

"What do you mean? I have been following you guys for the last two days! You mean, you didn't even know?" the little man began to dance around singing, "You didn't kn-o-w, you didn't- kn-o-w!"

"Who is this guy?" asked Kamarin puzzled.

Lort just shook his head.

"Why are you asking me?" said Erin.

"Why don't all of you come with me and maybe you'll find out." said the little stranger.

Swinging his oversized weapon over his shoulder, he started off in the same direction they were originally going. Then the little man stopped then turned and addressed them.

"I am Bugboody! King of the Great Granite River. Provider of all who thirst on L-2 and King of the Invisible Bridgers!" He stood proudly.

"And you are eight feet tall, as I am." Lort said laughing.

The little man's mouth clamped shut and he stared angrily at Lort. Then he turned his back to them and stomped his feet rapidly.

"Ugh! Oh! I think I have upset the little tike." said Lort.

The little man stopped suddenly and then leaped to one side. The ground shook as a large glass ball pushed up through the ground, through an opening that was camouflaged. It rolled and opened until only a half shell lay before them.

"Well...what are you waiting for? Get in!" The little King said as he himself jumped in.

"What is it?" asked Erin.

"It's a ballvator. Come on! Come on, we're late!"

Skeptically the others stepped in as the upper half of the glass ball slammed shut over them and they began to ascend up the side of the mountainous pillar. While the glass sphere rose, the valley looked as if they were looking through a fish eye.

It was almost too much for Erin. She overwhelmingly felt she was going to fall and held on to Lort's fur for dear life.

"Ouch! Missy, please don't pull so hard."

"I'm sorry, Lort, but it looks like we're falling!" She closed her eyes to ease her feeling of helplessness.

As the elevator came to a stop near the top of the rock spire, it changed direction and moved into what appeared to be a large cave.

Stepping from the glass bubble they could see hundreds of little people, running here and there on a large walkway that encircled the interior of the granite pillar.

Standing at a handrail Kamarin could see a shaft of light that beamed from the center of what appeared to be the ceiling. Looking down, there were many walkways with just as many little people on them doing much the same. The main floor was covered with tiny little people and was at least two hundred feet, possibly more, in diameter.

Suddenly and without warning like a disturbed hive of bees, their paces became lively. Little people were running into each other and brushing by them as if they did not exist. With an air of madness and smiling faces, they all ran to several large bulkhead- doors that dotted the perimeter of the granite walls. When the doors burst open, the answer to their madness became apparent.

Many Gorin fighters were buzzing the granite towers with strafing runs. While several close laser blasts exploded near the opening of the pillar wall, large guns came up from out of the deck floors separating the thick crowd of people.

Like a new form of entertainment, they fought each other for the gunman's seat. Skipping around laughing and yelling, it was a sure sign, that they were enjoying the fight as though it were a game.

One of the largest of the 'little men', made it to the seat and quickly powered up the weapon while some of the others continued to pull at him trying to dismount him to take his place.

Then, suddenly, several blasts from a Gorin fighter- fell just inside the gun deck sending a few of the little people out over the edge of the opening and to their deaths.

The little gunner feverishly began pushing and twisting knobs as the big gun rotated on its base, aiming out of the opening, the machine fired across the sky like flashes of lightening.

First one fighter disappeared in a puff of smoke, then two, then three. As the little people cheered with shrieks of joy, the Gorin fighters fell from the sky. And as quickly as it all started- it was over.

Though the targets had stopped coming, the barrage kept on for a minute or so. And when the excitement left, the little people were again silent as they went on about their business. All but one- and a handful of them were at work prying him from the controls as his adrenaline had taken over. When they succeeded, he had the molded face of a crazed man and the gun machine was lowered into the floor for the next invasion.

As the bulkhead doors were closed, Kamarin thought he saw something off on the horizon- but he too was still excited and expecting more.

Bugboody ran to them and stood at attention. "Did we do well?" he asked Kamarin.

"Ugh…Yeah, sure!" Kamarin replied.

"We are new at this sort of thing. We only just recently purchased all these anti-aircraft weapons when all of our neighbors were being attacked and killed. You see- we take care of our neighbors, we build bridges for them and keep the waters safe for their use. All of this we did for them and they did not even know that we existed. Because- we hide very well. But now they are all gone. Our efforts have been in vain. They are all dead now. We have a need to be useful and if we can, we will see an end to these invaders. We will continue to be helpful or I am not BUGBOODY, King of all the Bridgers! I am expected to lead these people…they look to me for direction. That is why I invited you here. We seek to be in your allegiance. I wish for your approval to please allow us to help you fight the Gorin- our Guardian." He then bowed to Kamarin.

Kamarin looked to his friends with a smile and put his hand on the little King's shoulder. "Bugboody, King of all these great warriors, you are certainly welcome to join us in our fight against the evil Gorin."

The little man smiled from one ear to the other and then walked to a nearby rail overlooking the floor full of people below. Raising his hands above his head, they all stopped what they were doing to hear what their leader had to say.

"Listen! All you Bridgers, all you keepers of the valley and the Great Granite River- listen! All the women of the Great River people. Now you have an even greater purpose! The powerful Guardian of Orion has just invited us to share in the fight against the terrible Gorin invaders!"

The little people cheered and became very active again. They danced and sang what must have been their anthem. It was a celebration of the largest kind. One little man suddenly ducked down behind Lort as two others leaped to his chest knocking him over onto his back. Lort was furious and jumped to his feet with one of the little fellas held by his neck. The little man gulped trying to swallow, giggling at the same time, unsure of Lort's next move.

"Lort, stop! Let the little one go!" said Erin.

Kamarin just snickered.

But Lort was not smiling when he loosened his grip, letting the little man fall and then turned and walked away grumbling.

As the evening went on, Bugboody and his mate gave Kamarin and Erin a tour of their granite tower while Lort found a corner to sit in to avoid stepping on the little people and to rest his feet and his pride.

Erin could see a small stairway leading to a hatch at the top of the tower.

"Does that door lead to the outside?" she asked Bugboody's little wife.

"Yes, it does. But I don't go up there because there are no hand rails and I am very afraid of heights," she said, backing away slightly to show her seriousness.

"Kamarin, would you please take me up there? I want to see it," she said already half out of her machine.

"Sure!" Kamarin said as he lifted her up and out.

Erin could feel all eyes were upon her as the little people stared at her waist and missing legs.

"It doesn't hurt you know," she said with a little smile and held onto Kamarin as he started the climb.

Kamarin slid the steel hatch open and revealed the brightly burning stars. In fact, they were so bright they were washed in a bluish haze.

Stepping onto the deck above, they felt almost one with the stars.

"We have to go home, Kamarin," said Erin.

"I know," he said. "But where is home?"

"Thelona, that's where."

"It doesn't exist anymore, Erin."

"It does exist, it does!" she exclaimed.

"Erin- Tessa told me all about our home planet before she died. It was blown up. She saw it with her own eyes. She always said that it was the end of the beginning."

"So you say my mother lied to me?"

"No, Erin, I did not say that. She might have been mistaken though."

"Kamarin, you are older than me but you aren't too bright."

"Well, I like that."

"My mother came to L-2 just before I was born. Couldn't it be possible that she might have known something your parents did not?"

"Possibly. But why didn't they ever come for us if they were still alive?"

"Maybe they couldn't. Maybe they didn't know that we had survived the war?"

"Yes, but word of what has happened here surely would have reached them by now. I am sorry, Erin, but I just can't believe in something that is just not possible. You've got to face it, it's just you and me."

Kamarin looked up trying to make his eyes focus on their home star system, imagining what awaited them there.

Erin laid down her head, and could almost make out the end of the river off in the distance. The water in the far distant delta shimmered in the reflection of the stars. Dreaming of her mother and praying for the end of the Gorin supremacy, she fell asleep.

Kamarin sat beside her and was almost mesmerized by the beautiful evening skyline. From their perch high above the valley floor, the curvature of L-2 could be seen. It was also quite a bit warmer at this elevation away from the frosty valley floor. He felt a little lonely even with his new found friends. He felt as if he were living someone else's life. I have not changed, he thought, but who am I? He suddenly felt strange. He would soon have to leave his only home he had ever known. But the urge he felt to leave was even stronger now. The need for him to be somewhere else was intense. He felt strongly that if he did not find a way to leave L-2 soon, the universe as they knew it would be destroyed. Where are the Gorin now, and who would be their next victims? He could not let anymore people die. He had made his decision- he should leave alone in the morning and search for Voltar.

He layed down next to Erin to give her some of his own heat, he did not notice his wristband with his arm draped over her, but if he had, he would have noticed the band was pulsating with a faint glowing red.

The next morning, there was an apparent lull between winter storms and it was now quite warm, especially at the top of the granite towers.

Kamarin woke to a warm breeze blowing across his face. Erin's contented look on hers, revealed she too, enjoyed the warm rays of the sun. Kamarin stood and stretched to get his blood to flow again. He was not prepared for what he was going to see next.

When he bent over to give his back a good stretch, opening his eyes as he was upside down, he suddenly raised upright again to get a better look at the huge Gorin ship hovering on the horizon.

It was the largest ship he had ever seen. It hovered slowly over the sea beyond the end of the river and was slowly making its way up the delta, heading for the river valley.

The Gorin battleship stopped periodically as it scanned for life signs. Kamarin turned to Erin and gently, but most urgently, shook her to wake her.

"Come on, Erin, wake up, we've got to go!"

"What's going on? Why are you...?" she said, rubbing her eyes until she, too spotted the menace.

Kamarin started down the opening of the stairs, for a brief moment, forgetting to consider Erin's handicap.

"Kamarin, wait!"

He quickly turned and scooped her up in his arms and headed down the stairs.

"How could you?" she said angrily.

"I didn't mean to leave you there alone- I'm sorry."

"You just don't care about me."

"I do, Erin, but sometimes I forget that you cannot walk."

"Oh! Then how do you see me?"

Kamarin suddenly felt trapped, "Right now we have more pressing matters, Erin."

"Well, what did you mean?" Erin's priority was her own curiosity.

"Please! Later, OK?" was all he said.

Kamarin carried her down and to her treader machine.

"Kamarin, what's going on?" she yelled to him as he ran around the walkway.

"Come with me!" said a voice from behind her. Someone was pulling on her arm. When Erin looked around, there was Bugboody's wife in a panic.

"Come quickly, we have to go to the underground!"

"Why, what's going on?"

"Two large spacecraft are outside and we do not know who they are or what they want, so please hurry!"

"No! I want to be with my friends and they are the enemy to the Gorin. Of course you know that though don't you?"

Pulling her arm free and dashing off, trying not to run over any little river people, she went to find Lort. When she did, he was huddled in a corner asleep. She also noticed his hair had returned to its more natural state of dark brown and that made it difficult to find him lieing down of course.

"Wake up, Lort!"

"What is it, little missy?"

"They've found us!"

"Where is the Guardian?" Lort asked.

"So you do admit that he is…"

Lort bent down and held her by the arms and looked her straight in the eyes.

"Missy! Tell me where he is if you can."

"I don't know, Lort, he ran down that way!"

It would have been easy to spot Kamarin if he still was inside the granite pillar because of his height. His friends did not see him take the elevator back down to the desert floor. He was now hastily making his way toward the craft through the cover of the valley's underbrush.

He knew that he was the only reason for the Gorin even being there. With any possible luck he would have the chance to end it all right here, he thought. But Kamarin was unnerved by the size of these large spaceships the Gorin possessed. His senses made him maintain his caution.

As he closed the distance on the Gorin craft, his wristband was glowing, bright blue.

Looking up from the heavy shrubbery giving him his cover, he was afraid that they would see it pulsating.

The ship hovered very low now and Kamarin could see several hatches in the underside. He only wished that he were tall enough to reach one of them. Maybe one would allow him access to the inside. The best way to see to it that the ship was destroyed would be from there, he thought. Still, he wondered how he could get up to it. Deke! Of course! He could grow large enough and raise him to it.

He quickly snatched Deke from his headband and placed him on the ground just under the Gorin warship. The metal man's light turned blue as it began to grow.

Suddenly the ship left them to hover over one of the granite pillars, which so happened to be where he had left his friends. A veil of light radiated down from its center engulfing the huge rock spire.

Kamarin, fearing for his companions, ran out into the open, yelling and waving his arms in a self-sacrifice. He was not surprised when a small ball of light came from the enemy ship directly at him.

Just before it would have made contact with him, he dove to the side, rolling as it exploded where he was standing.

He stood with a jump and snapped the other metal man from his wristband.

Deke looked down at Kamarin, making sure he had not been injured, and as if he awaited an order to counter attack. The metal man was almost as large as one of the granite towers now and the other metal man had grown to almost the same height, but with a sleeker look to his build. They had both taken on completely different shapes than that of which Deke had appeared to him years before. Kamarin had noticed subtle changes in their appearances at different sizes, but now they were significant. Their skin was still shiny smooth and glistened in the sunlight.

Both of his metal men stood at attention ready to fight. When Kamarin gave the command to advance, Deke stepped away, leaving Kamarin behind.

As Kamarin ran to catch up, he glanced around but had lost sight of his other metal man. He did not understand. He was there a second ago. Kamarin looked around and then from above came a shadow. He looked up and saw that the other metal giant had taken to the air and was heading for the Gorin ship. His now weightless metal man hovered next to it.

Kamarin reached into his pack and found a Landwheel and threw it at the generated light field surrounding the granite tower.

It exploded but had no effect.

The lighter than air metal giant cocked it's from head from side to side as it sized up the situation. Then it gave the Gorin battleship one quick punch!

The huge ship wavered a bit and the light field went out.

Kamarin watched with a smile but did not see the new threat that was now standing behind him. His hair on the back of his neck rustled. He turned swiftly then froze. It was as tall as Deke, almost his mirror image but without his jovial personality. This new giant had a threateningly different look about it. It had a dull finish to its outer skin, to the point that it seemed to absorb light around it. It almost seemed transparent, like it might not really be there.

But when it lifted its foot as if it were going to squash a bug, Kamarin decided that it probably was him that he planned to step on, and he had better move.

The ground shook jarring him to his knees again. This was no mirage.

As he ran from his cover in the tall thicket, he could see little people running from their granite towers to engage the many Gorin soldiers that were beginning to take up positions in the desert valley.

The giant invader came at Kamarin again but was met with a sudden jolt of resistance as his flying metal man crashed into his chest, knocking him to the ground.

Deke returned and started pounding on the enemy giant's head as it lay there.

The flying metal man returned to help Deke in the annihilation.

Deke picked it up over his shoulder and slammed it to the ground.

It suddenly raised up and went for Deke with a fury. It seemed to have a boost in its power and started its destruction by giving Deke a shock to his head, knocking him to the ground.

Kamarin searched for Erin and Lort in the skirmish that was taking place at the giant pillar's base. After he had destroyed two Gorin soldiers he spotted Lort swinging his hammer as he was pulverizing all those whom were brave enough, or dumb enough, to attack him.

Behind him, Erin was firing her laser pistol as fast as she could, making sure she did not hit Lort.

Lort spotted Kamarin, too and yelled to him, "Get behind me Guardian!"

As the Gorin foot soldiers and the river people fought, Kamarin and his friends, were all sort of an audience to one of the most titanic fights ever.

Then yet another giant intruder had joined in the match against Kamarin's metal men, this one very similar to the first.

The battle continued into the night. Thousands of little people struggled with the powerful enemy and hundreds of the little people were losing their lives.

But the Gorin, were too. They were suffering a heavy loss.

Suddenly a loud high pitch followed by a humming sound came from the two Gorin warships. Within a few minutes the enemy disappeared along with their two giants.

Deke had reduced in size and appeared on Kamarin's headband without damage, but the other's power slowly faded away from him as he slowly lowered himself down before Kamarin. It moved no more as it lay in front of him.

Kamarin was now feeling a power deficiency himself and stumbled over to the metal man's side and sat down.

Erin rolled, with her machine, over to join him.

"Kamarin, what were those things?" she asked.

"I don't know, they came from out of nowhere! My mother said nothing about them."

Kamarin then laid back against the metal man that was no longer functioning.

Lort climbed over the metal hulk to get to his friends.

"Guardian!" Lort said. "Did you see what happened just before they left?"

"No, I was not able to see much of anything."

"Well, I did! A bright light shone down from their ship and the ones fighting your metal giants just disappeared into it. It was as if they were sucked into the enemy's airship!"

"I don't understand," Erin said, as she put her head into her arm and leaned against the metal giant. "Kamarin, does this mean what I think it might?"

"Possibly."

"But how? I thought holographs were merely images made with mirrors?"

"I don't know, Erin. What I do know is that now we have a much larger problem on our hands. These new weapons of the Gorin are very formidable and now I am left with only one metal man. I am not sure that I still can be of any hope to anyone anymore."

"Well, if not you, than who can be? There is still hope, Kamarin. We are not dead yet, are we?" Erin said with a grin.

"What's so funny?" asked Kamarin.

"Do you know how many Guardians there were in the old war?" said Erin.

"Yes, there were five. But what does that have to with?"

"So, if you were to acquire the other Guardian's metal men, do you think that you would then be strong enough to defeat the Gorin?"

"Well…yes! But there remains one small problem."

"And what is that?" Erin asked, smiling as if something still was tickling her.

"No one knows where they have been hidden!"

"Kamarin, let me tell you why I had come to look for your parents. My mother told me many things that I really did not understand when I was young, but now I think I do. The last things my mother told me were that I should find your parents and convince them to help. I was supposed to tell them of the places where the secrets to Orion were kept- the lost gifts of the Orion people. Kamarin, I believe it is where the metal men are hidden until a Guardian could some day free his people from the evil Gorin. Kamarin, I know where they are!"

"Then what are we waiting for? Let's go and find them before it's too late." he said, as he gathered what few things he had with him, to leave immediately.

"No, Kamarin, you do not understand, they are not here on L-2," she said.

"Not here…then where are they?"

"We will need a ship, Kamarin!"

"With all of the destruction the Gorin have inflicted, where do you suppose we might find one?"

No sooner did Kamarin finish his question then something awesome took place. A hole suddenly appeared in the neck of the giant metal man and a faint light shown from inside.

"But I thought it was destroyed," Erin whispered.

She was not the only one surprised. Kamarin was sure it had been destroyed when he saw what he thought was the life drain from it just moments before. When they got a closer look however, he saw that familiar blue light emanating from deep within.

Kamarin gave his pack to Erin to hold and climbed in to take a look.

However curiosity was too much for her and she had Lort pick her and her machine up and place her into the hole. She was then able to move around quite easily inside because of a walkway that ran through bulkheads and far into the metal man's chest.

There she found Kamarin sitting in one of two seats that were facing a strange console and he was busy putting on a strange helmet he'd found. She just watched in awe as he fitted it.

Lort barely pulled his large frame into the opening. As he bent down to pass under the first bulkhead, he looked back and saw that the hole was no longer there!

Suddenly feeling trapped, Lort jumped back to the spot where he had just entered the metal man. Clenching his huge fist he started pounding on the inside of the metal composite skin. But it was solid and no door was there anymore one that he might have been able to open. Deciding that there was no immediate way out, he went on to find his friends.

Erin watched as Kamarin inspected the helmet attached to his chair by an umbilical.

He sat back into the plush seat that automatically fitted itself to his contour. Putting the helmet on again, he was miffed at the fact he could not see anything when he had it on. Then by accident he found when he sat back further into the chair, a picture appeared before his eyes. Inside the face shield, he could see everything that was outside the metal man. Kamarin knew then what was going on and how it worked.

He took the helmet off again and told Erin to park her machine next to him and checked to see where Lort was now. When he finally made it into the room, Kamarin anxiously pointed for him to sit down.

"You want me to sit here?" Lort asked, pointing to an undersized chair that obviously would not hold him. "I do not think it is large enough for me, Guardian."

Just then the chair changed its shape to accommodate the Granite man's girth.

Kamarin smiled. "Please, Lort, be my guest and try it. It looks quite comfortable to me."

As Lort moved closer to it, it changed a little more to compensate for his bulk. When he finally sat down, the seemingly alive-seat moved more to fit him like a glove. With a contented grin, Lort gave away the fact that he was enjoying the feel of the soft imitation leather.

"Where are we going?" Erin asked, when she finally understood why they had been invited into the metal giant.

"I don't know for sure, I thought you did." Said Kamarin.

Erin shrugged her shoulders.

"Well, at any rate, the last time I had the helmet on, I noticed that we had left L-2!"

"I felt nothing," said Lort.

"Me either," Erin added.

Kamarin just smiled, sat back, and put the helmet back on to see if he could tell where they were going.

When he turned his head from side to side, he could see out each side of their new spaceship. If he kept his head turned, the entire chair would move in the same direction until he could see behind them, and where they had come from.

"This is quite exciting!" Erin said, "But what about the little river people?"

"Well- they have a purpose now. I suppose they will keep fighting the Gorin if they return. Or the Gorin find out that we are no longer on the planet," said Kamarin.

"But the Gorin will destroy them!" Erin worried.

Kamarin could not answer her because he too was afraid for their new friends.

Their ship circled around L-2.

They were all silent while they remembered the little people and their fearless leader, Bugboody. Kamarin and his new friends reflected on their past and the people in their lives on L-2. It was hoped that they would all be left in peace now. And now that he was no longer on the planet, the Gorin should follow them far away.

Erin took the helmet from Kamarin and put it on.

"Hey!" Kamarin wondered what she was doing since she obviously did not see the other one attached to the back of Lort's chair. Kamarin reached for it and gave it to her, reclaiming his own. "Here!" he said, helping her with it.

"Kamarin, why haven't we left L-2 yet? We're still in orbit!" said Erin.

"Maybe he doesn't know where we want to go."

"How are we going to tell him?"

As they cruised around the planet, the solar winds, which were quite strong, carried them over many cities that were on fire now and burning with destruction; huge fires that slowly began to engulf the surface of L-2.

Kamarin took his helmet off.

Erin soon did the same and she cried. She cried tears for the many cultures that were lost. Many of them good. Most of them she had known and loved. The beings that gave the little mining planet life, were now gone. L-2 was soon left a lifeless rock on fire in space.

As the three defenders of Orion fell asleep, the metal man drifted away from L-2 and all of its memories.

"Five"

Today he looked perfect in all his attire, dressed in the finest uniform he could have made. All others who marched in the city center were dressed in shiny black. But being decorated in white and platinum would surely make him stand out for all to see at the head of the procession.

With the threat of the Guardians being able to suppress the inevitable Gorin dominance, Ogel and the evil Voltar were now being received as heroes, marking another milestone in Gorin history. Even though they could not produce the bodies of their enemy, the destruction of their hideaway proved to be enough to regain public confidence. The destruction of L-2 was a sweet taste of yet one more conquest. The loss of the raw ore that had been a source of fuel for their ships was not a problem. For now they had a new and even more powerful fuel that, because of Voltar, was easily produced synthetically. And with his new invention, they were able to design new and more powerful warships.

Spacecraft were being built in huge factories in four of their major cities, Aumundfaught, Hiesil, Ech'ball and Gorin Emuch Five. These factories were huge buildings over a thousand feet high and stretched over two miles in diameter. The Gorin cities were all interconnected due to the planet's population. The planet Gore was, in easier terms, a city within a city. And all of this, Voltar wished to rule again without any competition.

Voltar only lacked some vision, for he could not see that the position he lusted for was also being sought by the powerful, envious creature he was helping to create.

Ogel was a man born and raised with nothing, and now thirsty for all the power and wealth he could acquire. In this respect he could have been Voltar's son, Ogel thought as he marched. As he was with his own father, he would not have an ounce of remorse over Voltar's death. In fact, it was an option in Ogel's plan to someday take Voltar's place.

Ogel continued to play out different scenes of his grandiose take over as leader of the mighty Gorin. There would be only one hero, one God, and that would be him.

At the end of their long march the city's capitol, the chance also for Ogel to display his strong allegiance to the people's bureaucrats. His actions today would cement his relationship with them and once again prove his necessary position.

Voltar and Ogel stepped onto a large platform, presenting themselves for all to admire. The soldiers were assembled in formation facing the crowd below them. And beyond were thousands upon thousands of Gorin people gathered for the festivities. Nothing was mentioned but everything was understood, as the multitude roared their appreciation.

Then with his voice mysteriously amplified Voltar spoke…

"The enemy has been destroyed! None of the so-called Guardians exist anymore! Since the Great war I have pursued these people of my homeland and I have now conquered them. Now we can go on with our conquest of space. And Orion will answer only to us!"

Of course, he could be mistaken, but the cheers from the crowd clouded his mind from any other thoughts. Voltar turned and left the stage but Ogel stayed, lost in the illusion the applause was for him.

Ogel had nothing left to fear as he sipped his drink in one of the many clubs inside one of the many large buildings used mainly to house hundreds of Gorin families, if one could call them "families". More distinctly, the Gorin lived together for only one purpose, and that was to raise more of their own kind-'killers. If one Gorin partner lost his or her life in battle, it was not long and they would be living with another. No grieving was necessary. There was not any love lost because they knew nothing of love.

Most of the Gorin, were desensitized by the promise of an illusion- brought to life by their leaders, and nurtured by Voltar. He presented no threat to Ogel physically, for he was old and scarred from many battles. But what bothered him the most, was where were Kamarin and his fighting metal men? He would feel more confident of his position if he knew that Kamarin was really dead. He knew that if Kamarin was still alive and was any resemblance to his parents, he could be facing a very determined foe.

Ogel was aware of Kamarin's metal men, yes indeed, since of course, his little escapade with Kamarin in the desert. But Ogel also knew that where Kamarin wore his heart it made him all too vulnerable. That would be the key to his demise. Ogel remembered how Kamarin was always such a bleeding heart.

Ogel laughed to himself with a jealous anger. He would not rest until Kamarin was finished.

"You still are the center of attraction, Kamarin! Even when you are dead!" Ogel said as he squeezed his glass until it shattered in his hand. And as if nothing was wrong, he quietly got up and left the club.

Unlike Ogel, having so much surplus energy, Voltar retired to his quarters, for a rest and service. Oh yes, service. In a battle some years before and after the great one, he had almost been killed, and was hospitalized. His attack vehicle he had been riding in was hit by enemy fire and suddenly exploded under him, killing everyone else but him. He would have died because of the large amount of blood he had lost but his medical team saved him with a transfusion. Unfortunately for Voltar, what was good blood for the Gorin, was almost incapacitating to him. The only blood available was from an alien Augerite infected with an incurable disease that attacked the liver, of only humans. His only means of survival would be to infuse himself with a machine that cleansed his blood and added antibodies to fight the cursed infection.

When he felt his body, start to swell, he would plug himself in by means of a quick disconnect fitting installed in his side.

With his body imprisoned, tethered with the umbilical, Voltar reclined into his plush easy chair and watched the moons outside his small window appear on the Gorin horizon. The light from them gleamed off the many metal buildings between his room and the firmament of the planet. In these solemn times he found himself missing the beautiful horizons of his home planet, beautiful Thelona. But with his life that he had long since chosen, they would be forever just memories. That sector of Orion was forbidden, even to himself now. Besides, he felt it was better that way.

Voltar also had a hard time adjusting to the gross anatomies of his hosts of this world. With their low foreheads, beady eyes, large ears and stubby bodies they dearly lacked for beauty.

He was not the type who needed a mate most of the time but he could appreciate some visual contact with a woman of his own kind now and then. But slaves were off limits.

The women of Thelona were not all the same and their gentle nature was admirable. He almost hated himself when he began to entertain thoughts such as these. But then how could he hate himself when everyone loved and revered him? Ah, but Gorin women- if you could call them women! Maybe if he was able to tell them apart from their men. No matter, it was all just entertaining thoughts anyway.

Remorsefully, at times, he wondered though if he would ever see his homeland again. He wondered, too if he might feel again. He had managed to loose the

93

ultimate control he once had had. And without a healthy young body to house his ingenious mind, what hope could he possibly have of regaining it. For now he would use the young Ogel like a puppet that would eagerly work his dastardly deeds and then he would simply put him to death. For now he would live, until he has helped him get rid of his rival and helped him gain control of the galaxy. Then he would have the young Olgel preserved in a block of ambersite, to allow the Gorin people to pay their respects to their young and handsome alien hero.

"Six"

The metal giant carried no combustible fuels. In order to move through the air and space, he used a form of a magnetic pulse fluctuation to pull and repel himself. His powerful power plant in his chest would generate a strong magnetic field to his exterior skin, when he flew and during battle. This too protected his occupants inside. The faster he moved through space, the faster he would be launched from planet to planet.

Most other spacecraft used an inner and outer hull to create a magnetic field to enable them to move through space, like a gyro in the air. They faced many problems due to mechanical breakdowns. Maneuvering in a planet's atmosphere, for example, due to their powerful magnetic field forces; they would be subject to slipping. Slipping came with the sudden change in direction, like a spinning top out of control, and would cause the space-craft to slam to the ground. Kamarin's metal men, on the contrary, were state of the art and needed no moving parts and therefore had no problems associated with the high torque presented by them. Therefore, the metal giant moved quite easily and was easily able to hover and change his direction in a flash.

So, with the same burst of energy as an atom being split, the metal man, with his three trusting passengers, sped through the solar systems toward Orion and ultimately towards their home.

Kamarin woke to find he was still wearing the helmet. Watching the stars streak by startled him a bit but he was pleased to see that they were still in transit. Even if he did not know their point of destination.

Taking the helmet off, he got up to stretch and check on the others.

Erin was stirring and soon she would awake.

Lort laid sprawled out, almost covering his seat with his dangling legs and arms. He snored heavily.

"Go ahead and sleep, big fella, you've earned it," Kamarin said with a grin.

Slowly Kamarin became uneasy as he remembered he himself had little sleep due to the dream he had awakened from. After watching the destruction of L-2, he fell into a deep sleep and envisioned his mother pointing to the evening sky as if she were excited and filled with an unexplained joy. He saw two planets side by side. One was so beautiful with colors of white with shades of blue and green. The other was dark as night. A strange man was leading him and his friends on some sort of a journey. Then the alarming feeling of fighting the Gorin washed over him. Could his mother have known more than she had told him? Or was this a message from beyond? Then came an audible voice while he thought of his visions.

"Listen, Kamarin!"

It was startling and echoed in his mind. He turned to see who was talking to him but the voice was not Erin's. No one else had heard it but him, so he eased back into his seat with a numb feeling.

"What's wrong?" Erin asked.

"Nothing really- except we should be there shortly."

"Where's there?"

"Home, I should guess. I don't know of any other place."

"Home doesn't exist anymore remember Kamarin?"

"Well, he seems to know where he is taking us so I guess we should just enjoy the ride."

"What's to enjoy, I don't feel any movement and I can't even see outside!" Erin complained.

"I know this is not real entertainment but it is transportation!" Kamarin sat back down and closed his eyes and hummed a little. "Just relax Erin—Aughh! I'm going to."

Erin, feeling impatient, put her helmet back on. "Ugh- Kamarin!"

"Hugh?"

"I think we're there!"

Kamarin quickly righted himself and grabbed his helmet. "What strange planet is this? Where are we?"

They both sat on the edge of their seats as they observed a pink-ish colored planet that they were now in orbit around.

"I saw nothing like this in any of my dreams nor did my mother ever speak of it."

"What do you mean?" asked Erin.

Kamarin was a little shocked when he heard her through the earphone in his helmet.

"Hugh? Oh- I'll tell you later. What is going on? The battle must have done something to his memory! I mean- this looks nothing like any of the worlds my mother told me about. I thought it knew where we had to go."

"Maybe he does. He might know better than we do," Erin said as she maneuvered her track machine down the walkway to the same place where they had entered through the metal man's skin.

"Where do you think you're going?" Kamarin asked.

"If you would pay more attention, you would have noticed that we have landed."

Lort's feet thumped to the floor, realizing what was taking place. He was a little upset because Erin did not wake him.

Kamarin could see Erin watching as the hole slowly appeared, washing her in a bright light from outside.

Looking out, they surveyed a desert-like planet with a pink-ish haze on the horizon, no doubt caused from the peculiar colored sand.

As they climbed from the metal man and stood on its strange surface, the sand was a powdery dust, surrounding and clinging to their feet as they walked.

The flying metal man came to life again after changing back to a more familiar shape and stood at attention as if it were on guard. Why did it bring them to this planet Kamarin thought. His mother never told him of this or in fact any other planet with a similar design. It indeed was a mystery. But the question now was, what now? He knew nothing of this place.

Kamarin turned and addressed the metal man.

"Tell me, why did you bring us to this place?"

"Does he talk, too?" Erin asked as she carefully studied the metal man's face.

"No! Of course he cannot!" Kamarin said as he kicked the sand at his feet in frustration.

"Does this mean that we are lost?" Lort asked as Kamarin and Erin passed a stare at him.

While Kamarin kept Lort entertained and metaphorically went on about their hopeless situation, Erin busily investigated their new surroundings.

"I don't think we're lost. Kamarin, look at that planet over there." Erin said pointing off into the horizon. "Doesn't it look familiar?"

"Are you kidding?" asked Kamarin.

"Think, Kamarin- doesn't it look like Skyberia?"

Kamarin studied the planet that was really very close. It was more than apparent that it was much larger than the one they were on. Yes, it did fit his mother's description of their home planet's twin. Since this one was large enough and colorful enough, it invariably convinced him of it.

As they began to walk through the desert towards a mountain range, which seemed to be their next destination, he believed that this planet was probably one of Skyberia's moons.

The passing day brought the planet on the horizon into full view. But still a more chilling sight came with the appearance of yet another planet farther from the first. This one seemed to have had its life's light extinguished. It was not hard to see that the other was the sister planet to the first. And more over, Kamarin knew what it was now he was looking at and suddenly he could not breathe.

"Thelona!" He said.

The sight of it brought Kamarin to his knees. And he wept. He was thankful his parents were not able to see it. The darkened planet appeared as a tomb for all whom had perished there, a tombstone to remind others of the Gorin terror.

Kamarin stood slowly until he was as tall as he could stand with the rage that filled him. As if energized, he raised his arms and yelled into the sunset sky.

"Creator of all! Give me strength now! For I-Kamarin Mitchel- GUARDIAN of Orion, keeper of my mother's metal men and now orphan of Thelona, vow with every breath I take and with all the strength that I have, to end this madness and to see the evil Voltar pay for his evil deeds. He will be as lifeless as the people of my homeland his 'light' will be as dark as the night that now shrouds our beloved Thelona. MOTHER- Your Guardian is strong, and you and father will be avenged!"

With no immediate danger and all seeming to be quiet, the metal man who had brought them to this moon, reduced again in size and appeared in a flash on Kamarin's wristband.

They traveled far through the desert on foot and now were high into the mountainous range.

The three of them were now chasing a halo of light that shown from the top of a mountain and grew brighter as they got closer to it.

The mountain's side became very steep towards the top and in most areas Lort had to help Erin in her machine when its tracks slipped in the loose rock. But soon it was impassable for her and they were forced to stop and assess the situation.

Above them the rays of light coming from the top shimmered over the jagged rock wall, separating them from their destination. It all seemed adequately protected. An army would not be able to penetrate this place easily.

"Kamarin, you go on. I can't keep up with you," Erin said.

"That's all right, Erin. I'll stay with you and we can try again tomorrow."

Erin could see in his eyes that Kamarin really wanted to continue on but for her sake would give up the trek forward.

"I won't hear of it Kamarin. Besides, Lort will stay with me and I will be quite safe as always. Now go on-you must see what is the source of that light."

"She's right, Guardian. Nothing will harm her or you, as I will guard you both with my life. If you want to climb the rock, you have that right, and I will listen for you to call me if I am needed, for it is not far to the light. Now go, for I believe as she- we- need to know more about its source."

Kamarin began to climb. It was precarious but not a long climb for him and he easily was able to quickly reach the top and wave to his friends before he pulled himself over the wall. On the other side of the ground was covered by a rich layer of green grass.

Venturing further, many flowers and assorted plant life slowed him in his pace. No where else on this mountain were there so concentrated and seemingly arranged plant life in all of it's floral majestic design.

When he finally broke through the foliage, he looked down onto a small basin within the mountain peeks. Like a garden from heaven it was picture perfect with at least five small waterfalls feeding into a large pond at the center, beneath a shroud of trees was a little cabin with a big spotlight of blue curiously aimed to the sky.

Kamarin partially hid himself and waited to see who it was who lived in this secluded oasis. As he watched the small hut, he noticed the blue light slowly dropped over until it flooded the ground below.

Then to Kamarin's delight, a man appeared in a long white robe and started to diligently work to adjust the weakly-mounted search-light while he mumbled to himself. He had long white hair and wrinkled white skin. The light suddenly fell again and blinded the old man and he quickly jerked at the power supply cord until it jammed itself into place again. Holding his hand over his eyes he retreated into the confines of the hut. But then he appeared again and looked in Kamarin's direction.

"If you are hungry and mean me no harm, you are welcome to join me." Briefly waiting for an answer, he closed the curtain to the hut's entrance behind him.

How could he have seen him? He was hidden by the darkness of the night and plant life. But the invitation could not have come at a better time for he realized that his stomach was growling loudly. Could it have been? No, he thought.

Kamarin lowered himself down the steep, grassy slope he was on by holding onto the many branches. He only briefly wondered who this reclusive gentleman might be. They had come far, and he was tired and hungry. Maybe he could bring something to his friends.

He had to be alone the hut he was living in was only large enough to house one person. The door was covered with only a thin fabric so it was evident he did not feel in danger of any marauders.

When Kamarin stepped inside, the aroma of the food being served hit him in the face. It was wonderful. The old man had his back turned to Kamarin as he moved hurriedly around a boiling pot. Stirring its contents, he worked with enthusiasm to season it with various spices. Then he walked over to a large steel container in the corner and popped off the lid. High pitched chattering came from inside. As he watched, the old man took a large pair of prongs from a hook and fished for whatever was inside. When he pulled out the thing he had trapped in the pinchers, he quickly threw it into the boiling pot. It was long and slithery.

Surely he wasn't going to eat that, Kamarin thought as his hunger pains were now confused.

"Don't worry," he said as he turned and looked up at Kamarin. "It's quite good really."

He poured some of the soup into two bowls and sat down at a small table, motioning him to do the same. Kamarin took a chunk of the gelatinous meat and popped it into his mouth. Before he could even think of rejecting it, the glob slid down his throat. The taste however wasn't too bad. But the texture required some getting used to. Kamarin's quirky grin revealed his thoughts.

"Ha! Ha! Ha! It took me over twenty years to get used to it," he said as he chuckled, "You are Thelonan aren't you?" he asked.

"How did you know that?"

"Because there are no humans on this rock and the only ones who do occasionally visit are traders or vagabonds. And you have the appearance of neither.

"Hmm! Well, who do I look like then?"

"Might I be mistaken—you resemble someone that I have been waiting for."

Kamarin was shocked. How could this man know of him? Was this some sort of a trick? "What do you mean, sir?"

"Well, I'm sure you did not just happen upon the adornment you are wearing. That shawl is the work of a Thelonan woman, a ruling class woman. And you are most likely her relative, son, I would wager by your age. And there is no one else I know you could be except- the new GUARDIAN!"

Kamarin suddenly started choking. The stranger kindly patted him on his back.

"There, there, now! You have to watch those meat chunks, sometimes they catch you by surprise."

"Who are you, mister? How could you know all of this?" Kamarin asked, still catching his breath.

"My boy! I was the one who designed the metal figures your wearing!"

"But I thought that…."

"You thought we were all gone? Well, we are not! Most of us who played a role in creating the metal giants escaped to other planets along with thousands of others."

"Others?"

"Yes—others! Although our numbers have decreased some, most of our people fled safely to other planets throughout the galaxy. But they are afraid to return to Thelona without a Guardian to lead them."

"Return to Thelona? Old man, are you blind? Thelona is a burned out cinder which orbits your sun."

"Oh yes, that is what it is, of course," he said with a grin.

Kamarin began to wonder now if the confinement of this barren planet had not made him mad. "I have to go now," he said as he picked up his pack.

"Your Laith and Tessa's boy, aren't you?" the man asked suddenly and quite soberly.

Kamarin dropped his pack and slowly turned in amazement.

"How do you know these things, old man?" he asked.

"I was one of the people responsible for helping your parents escape. I do not know your name but I have been waiting for you to come for a long time. Your mother loved you very much, you know? She used to sing to you before you were born. Ah- yes! Your mother was so beautiful. A very lucky man your father."

"My name is Kamarin."

"She would—oh…Yes! Of course—pleased to meet you Kamarin, Kamarin Mitchel. You 'are' the

Guardian of Orion. Very pleased to meet you," he said, taking Kamarin's hand and shaking it.

Kamarin sat back down for a moment. He realized that this old man really was who he said he was. With all that information, he had to have been one of the council of the Ten.

As the man talked about the Great war and of Thelona, it reminded him of his mother and of how much she too loved her home. He explained that the few scientists that had worked on the Metal Man project had escaped, but most were now all dead. He had kept himself alive in hopes that he might someday return to Thelona.

Kamarin sat tight-lipped to allow him his allusion. But when the old man told Kamarin that there had been a few left behind during the war, and that two of them were also Guardians, he couldn't take anymore.

"Dreams! Old man, those are just dreams! Thelona was destroyed or didn't you hear me?" he said standing and pointing through a small window.

"Yes Kamarin, and that is also what the Gorin have thought for years. But 'that' is not Thelona. My dear boy- that is 'Skyberia'." he said, grinning from ear to ear.

Kamarin's chin dropped and his eyes widened as he felt himself go numb.

"I- I've got to go! But I'll be back!" he yelled as he bolted out of the door. "I have to bring my friends, so don't go anywhere! "Kamarin said suddenly overcome with excitement kicking up dirt as he disappeared over the hill.

"Where will I go?" the old man said out loud as he finished his soup, happy that his long exile was over.

Lort began to climb up the rock wall with Erin tied to his back.

Kamarin had already made it to the top again, and was urging Lort not to slip.

Lort's massive hands and feet were not made for rock climbing. But in any event, he wasn't about to be bested by this obstacle, if there was enough room for a finger or big toe, then he would cram it in and lift himself up. Thirty feet into the climb and Erin still had her face buried into Lort's fur.

Finally having made it to the top, Kamarin helped Erin and Lort pull her machine up to them with a rope. Her machine weighed at least two hundred and fifty pounds but Lort lifted it with ease.

Feeling catered to too much Erin pulled herself in and refused further help from either of them.

"One day I will not need this machine and you will depend upon me," she said as she once again zipped herself in. Even though if it were not for her 'Tredder' she would not have been able to have met Kamarin, she felt it a curse, and somewhat ashamed.

Lort lay in the lush green grass to rest outside the little hut after cleaning the pot of its soup. He dozed with the feeling of being full.

Erin was hungry, but could not bring herself to eat the main course.

So the old scientist offered her some fresh fruit instead. She made cooing noises as she enjoyed their sweetness.

"Sir, you have not told us your name," Kamarin said, trying to chew up some more gristle.

"I am Tresodin Koy. I frankly am surprised I have not forgotten it by now."

"Tell me Tresodin, how do you know that the dark planet is not Thelona?"

Caught with his mouth slightly full, and wiping his chin, "Well, it was unintentional really.

You see the Gorin had sent a handful of their fighters to Thelona to get a fixed position on our capital cities. We destroyed them all before they could relay any messages to the rest of their fleet. Their main armada was returning from Belladine after they had destroyed it. A good portion of our people had already gone to smaller planets in the galaxy to avoid annihilation. The last of us left in freighters accompanied by some of our warships. They spotted our group of space-craft close to Skyberia. We had no time to regroup after their fighters had begun to tear us apart. Three hundred and fifty ships tried to escape to the planet's surface but disappeared. Luckily for some of us, we were not followed and were able to escape.

Voltar, in all of the confusion in battle, directed his armies to destroy what he thought was Thelona simply because the majority of our ships tried to take refuge there. He has a great analytical mind but unfortunately for him, he has trouble thinking under pressure.

To this day I am not too sure he really knows what kind of huge mistake he had made. Hopefully God has clouded his mind," he said then burped.

"Is there any way to get our people back?" asked Erin.

"I'm afraid that they are too frightened. Because you see, the only Guardians that were left were killed in the battle on Skyberia!" Full now he sat back with a bloated look on his face.

"Then it is hopeless! We will never find the other metal men and be strong enough to destroy their new warships." Kamarin said feeling defeated.

"You do not realize the power you have been given, do you?" Tresodin said, obviously knowing more to Kamarin's becoming the Guardian, than they did. "Anyway, what new weapons are you talking about?"

"The Gorin seem to have a new weapon. They are not metal men but they seem to possess the same power," Erin answered while Kamarin walked around anxiously.

"Yes, they are strong and they are transparent," Lort added, popping his head inside the hut, wishing he could have dealt with them with his hammer. Lort let the curtain fall again and stayed outside to listen.

"Transparent, Hugh?" Tresodin thought as he played with his beard. "Voltar was working on some strange experiments with holograms before he was sent to Gore, you know."

"What kind of experiments?" asked Kamarin.

"It's evident you already know. He created images of light that could be used to do physical tasks." Tresodin rubbed his forehead and played with his eyebrows trying to remember events of long past, and the knowledge of the blue light power- given to the Thelonans by God 'himself'.

"Then that explains the light that they were followed by when they disappeared. We cannot fight this man, Voltar. He can create anything." Kamarin said as he felt further defeat.

"Oh please, Kamarin! You give Voltar way too much credit in these matters. Why do you think he was sent away in the first place?" Tresodin knew that Voltar hadn't the knowledge of the blue light gift.

"Why then was he?"

"Because the man was too clumsy. Most of his experiments failed and the Ten wanted to take his authority away because of his cynical attitude, but decided to give him another chance as Emissary to Gore."

"And he has been winning ever since as leader of the Gorin." answered Erin.

"He has had some failure with that too. And besides, he has never been able to get his hands on any of the metal men, and he won't. No, that he can never do. And I am the only one who knows where they are. Well, at least one of them. If I only knew how to get them after we find the place." Tresodin said with his fist clenched and pounding it on the table, trying to control his anger resurfacing in him.

"I know how to get them. Just show me where they are," Erin said proudly.

"What does she mean?" Tresodin looked at Kamarin and asked.

"Well it seems- that her mother had information as to how to retrieve the metal men if we could get to Thelona. Until now that was impossible!" Kamarin explained.

"Yep! My contribution all right," she said smiling, rocking back and forth at the waist in her machine.

Looking around the room they wondered where Lort was, then suddenly, he stuck his head inside the little hut again, startling them all as Tresodin began to laugh.

"Well, watch out Voltar, we're coming home! And what a team we will make." Kamarin said and they all began to laugh.

Except for Lort, he just smiled ear to ear.

-*-

After Tresodin had packed his belongings, they left the little hideaway and started the long descent for the desert plains again.

There, nothing much grew for the lack of proper soil and water, and many small planets could be seen in the sky above, because of their central location in the galaxy.

"Where are you taking us?" Erin asked Tresodin.

"To my home." He pointed with his walking stick.

"But I thought that place upon the mountain was your home."

"Well, that is where I spend most of my time lately, but it is not my home," he said as he marched through the sand with his white robe flowing in the breeze. "Actually, my plan was to stay there to either die or someday make contact again with my own people. I was very fortunate that you found me before I lost hope. I am very privileged to see a Guardian again. The creator of it all has his special reasons for everything and now I am able to be a part of it. I have been revitalized. Even Kamarin has no greater master," he said addressing Erin, "He knows he has been sent here by him to free Orion again. No person ever had such a task before him."

111

Erin felt compelled to get to know Tresodin and hopefully he would have more good news, maybe some good news for her.

"My mother often spoke of one who would save us. I did not know I would actually meet this person. I did not know Kamarin until a few months ago. My mother only told me of his parents and I feel I know them quite well, even if we have not met." Erin looked quite serious now.

"Were my parents also Guardians?"

"No, Erin, but I will say, that if it was not for your parents' help, all this would not have been possible."

"My parents died, you know?" she said, a little choked up.

"Yes, I do know, Erin, Kamarin told me and I am very sorry to hear of it." Tresodin could see the tears welling up in her eyes and cut short their conversation.

During their trek in the desert, Kamarin noticed they were on a direct course for a small sand-storm that was not moving.

A long time had passed and still it had not changed. When they came close to the wall of sand, he decided that they would have to go around it because of its intensity.

"Where are you going?" Tresodin yelled above the noise of the wind.

"Surely you can see we cannot go through this!" Kamarin tried yelling above the sound of the wind.

"I know what you think! But I am the one who put this here!" Tresodin said and covered his face and continued into the fierce sandstorm.

The others stood puzzled. Then when the Tresodin, didn't stop but wrapped a piece of cloth around his face, they did the same and followed him.

Kamarin gave Lort an end of a cord that he had kept tied to his waist, and quickly tied the other end around a hook on the front of Erin's machine, as they struggled to see in the blowing sand.

"Do not lose us!" Kamarin yelled, trying to keep Tresodin in sight.

"Do not worry!" was all he said just before he disappeared.

It was horrible! Sand blew hard into their faces. Kamarin definitely was unable to see where he was going but he pushed himself to walk on. Fortunately they did not have to go much farther, and when they broke through the old scientist was just standing there making sure they did not get lost.

After they had walked another fifty yards, they came upon a huge pit with a large clay house surrounded by many menacing mechanical devices. The machines were all in quite good working order, doing whatever it was that they were doing.

Tresodin explained how the machines were all interconnected and were responsible for making the dust storm to keep away intruders. The storm actually created a complete canopy over his home and grounds surrounding it. He went on to explain about how he had taken salvaged parts from crashed space-craft in the desert. He also said that most of the occupants gave up their treasures willingly. Some, on the other hand, needed persuasion. "Some unfortunately died trying to save them." he said with a smile.

113

"Where are the metal men?" asked Kamarin impatiently.

"Oh! Well they are not here."

"Then why have we come here?" Erin asked.

"Because of the type of transportation we will need to travel from here to Thelona without being discovered. They are under that covering over there. Go ahead and pull it off. Time is wasting away", he said motioning to Lort.

The giant Lort pulled the heavy cloth off of their new transports with one hand. "What are they?" he asked.

"Those are our one-way tickets home my friends." Tresodin said presenting them proudly.

"Are they space machines?" asked Erin.

"I don't understand. Are they supposed to grow?" Kamarin asked as he inspected five cylinders that appeared to once have been some kind of missiles of war.

"You have not read anything about your history, have you? I am disappointed. Well then, I will tell you.

Before the Gorin, Thelona used them in colonization experiments. They are transport pods."

"What do you mean they are our one-way tickets?" asked Kamarin.

"Well, the pods will see us safely through the planet's atmosphere and then softly to the ground but after that they will be of no use again. The pods will then be out of fuel and slightly damaged."

"Damaged?" Lort asked, suddenly very interested.

"Yes, big fella, but it has nothing to do with touchdown. It just means that when the pod deploys itself into the atmosphere, it looses some of its integral, as well as its exterior, parts in flight. Therefore," he patted the capsule causing it to echo, "making it impossible to travel through space again."

"It all sounds too archaic if you ask me. Why not use the metal man?" asked Kamarin.

"Because the Gorin have the twin worlds under close surveillance with many space probes. Any ship larger than these would leave a specter trail and would be quickly discovered by them. But with these little devils, we- will appear as simply a small hail of falling stars. Yes! Ha! Ha! Falling stars!"

As Tresodin relaxed in a chair that he brought out of his house, he began giving directions to Lort as to how to set up the pods. He lazily sipped from a glass, which contained an unknown fluid and seemed to be in danger of straining his finger as he busily pointed.

Each of the transport pods were slightly taller than Lort and only half again as wide, luckily for the group they would not have to leave him behind. In all reality, they would not even think of it.

Lort was busy standing each of the pods upright. Even though they were quite heavy, he was at home doing what he was born to do.

Erin could not possibly help with such a task but she had not seen Lort work so hard and felt the urge to. She was afraid he might drop one and hurt himself. Without concern for her safety, she instinctively raised her hands as if she would catch the heavy pods, if he were to lose his grip.

When Tresodin was through giving directions, he looked over his shoulder and saw that Kamarin was in his atrium garden, on one knee, and with head bowed facing his home Thelona.

-*-

That very night- they had all climbed into their respective capsules.

And as the effects of the launch finally wore off, Kamarin woke.

He looked for the others through his small porthole in front of him, but he was unable to see them. A slight panic brought him to move side to side. He twisted and in turned causing the pod to roll enough for him to see his friends hurtling along side.

Erin passed very close to his pod and he was able to make out her face. Her expression revealed a total enjoyment of the situation. Wide-eyed with an ear to ear grin. Her expression was so innocent that he could not hold back and he laughed happily for her.

When they came closer to Thelona, he could only imagine that his people must have been very content with life on this planet. Before they had been betrayed by Voltar.

It was so beautiful. Thelona had really survived the 'great' war!

Kamarin just could not understand the reasons for Voltar's treason, not now after looking upon the beautiful world he was from. He had everything he could want as did everyone else.

But now he had an army of destruction.

Most would feel a need to create and feel some sort of accomplishment only. With the same attitude of a spoiled child, he wanted and needed no one's love. Only his own exuberance of greatness was important to him. How selfish a man was he, It left little to be explained only wonder remained.

The only fact left, was that Voltar and his sidekick had to be stopped- even if it meant ending their lives.

Kamarin could now see the intense heat created from the atmosphere's effect on the capsules entering Thelona's space.

As the nose of his friends' pods became red, he knew his must be too, but no temperature change could be felt inside.

The small display panel under his chin could only be seen by looking at a mirror mounted above his head, throughout their entire flight, only the coordinates of their destination were displayed. But now it had begun to flash. No doubt they were coming close to the end of their trip. The gravity made his body shift slightly to his shoulders and he realized that he was speeding for the ground at over eight thousand miles an hour. Was this going to be his untimely end?

Suddenly several panels from the nose section blew off. Kamarin knew the pods were just too old

Then suddenly with a quick jerk, he was righted. Through his small window he could see the others had done the same. He could see large propellers had deployed and were now riding on the wind. He only wished that he could see now where they were going to land.

Sooner than he expected, the impact came as they touched down.

Catching his breath, for a moment he laid there awed by the beautiful sky above his porthole. The clouds were billowy, unlike any he had ever seen.

With the pressure equalization quickly completed, the pod's door hissed as it cracked open.

But as soon as it had opened, it was then slammed shut from outside.

Instinct took over as Kamarin hit the pod door with both hands.

The door opened slightly but again was shut on him. His heart began to race being unable to see who his attacker was.

Then suddenly he felt the pod being dragged. A large hand shown over the porthole. It was Lort! But why would he do this?

When they sopped, Kamarin shoved with all his might and fell halfway out of the pod.

"What do you think you are doing?" Kamarin yelled as he quickly pulled himself from the craft.

Lort was hunched over as if ready to fight.

For a moment it looked like the two were going to engage the other in battle.

But then Lort raised his finger to his lips and hushed Kamarin to be quiet and looked over some large rocks to a clearing beyond.

Kamarin was charged but turned inquisitive in an instant.

There was a platoon of Gorin fighters coming over a far away hill towards them.

"So that's it, Hugh?" said Kamarin, more at ease.

"Yes Guardian, I am sorry but there was little time to explain. When you did not get out of your transport right away, I thought you were unconscious so I did what I had to. I spotted them from the air but I do not think they saw us."

Kamarin could see that his friends had landed safely at the edge of the forest they were now in. He, on the other hand had touched down in the lush, green, grassy fields of beautiful rolling hills beyond. Lort had dragged him at least a hundred yards to safety.

With every step the Gorin took, Kamarin's anger grew. This was his home. They had no right trespassing. The game was about to begin and it was his turn now.

It was night now and the Gorin invaders had set up camp on a hill very close to them next to the forest. Tresodin and Lort had finished reassembling Erin's treader, as it was necessary to bring it with them in her pod.

Tresodin had also brought with him life packs, very much like Kamarin's day- pack but without weapons. Each of them contained many useful items such as food, water, solar blankets and some small tools for other survival techniques. They would be needed if the group were to split up and meet with any peril.

When the last of Kamarin's friends fell fast asleep, it was time for him to go to work. He slowly and stealthily left the group and hid in the nearby underbrush. He prepared his face and hands with a pasty black substance he kept for occasions when he did not want to be seen. Tonight he would have to move very quietly so he could not use any of his explosive weaponry.

He again searched his pack for something else he had been saving, for this kind of opportunity. It brought back many memories as he slipped it from its cover. The very knife that Ogel had tried to kill him with in the desert on L-2 long ago, Olgel's Tonbouy.

Before he left to infiltrate the Gorin camp, he lowered himself to his knees and said a prayer asking for forgiveness for what he must now do.

Erin had heard something or at least she thought, as she was startled from her sleep. She could have sworn she heard a scream. But feeling very groggy still requiring more sleep, she listened as she dozed, for something else that might alert her but all was quiet. Gazing at the stars through the tree-tops she began to fall asleep again. Suddenly she jolted awake and saw Kamarin sneaking back into camp to lie down. What was he doing she wondered. Maybe it was a personal problem he had to deal with. She sighed and finally clamped her eyes shut. She eventually woke to the sounds of a crackling fire.

Kamarin was busy cleaning a small fish he evidently had caught somewhere close by.

"Kamarin! What are you doing? Aren't you afraid that they might see the smoke from our fire?" Erin asked.

"The threat is now gone, missy!" Lort said, bending down to give her a handful of meat from another fish.

"Did they leave?" she asked- but no one spoke. "Well?" still there was no reply. "Kamarin, you have something on your face, what is it?"

Kamarin reached up and wiped his face and checked his hands to see if he had cleaned off all of the camouflage, but he noticed he had not.

"Kamarin, did you?" she asked.

"The Guardian protected us last night, Missy! He just did what he had to do," Lort interrupted.

"Why? We were not attacked."

"Exactly!" replied Kamarin, giving her some fish that was cooked and took the fish Lort gave her that was not.

"This war has affected us all, Erin," said Tresodin.

"What? Made us all into killers?" she countered.

"Kamarin now has great responsibilities. It will require the use of all of his talents. Some of those are better left unsaid," Tresodin said calmly, poking the fire.

Erin did not care for what had taken place, but she decided not to push it since she could not comprehend his action, even though it 'was' war.

"If everyone has had their fill, I suggest we get on our way," Tresodin raised his voice a little now, "The city in which both of your parents were born in is just through this forest. It's going to take us all day to get there so we should make haste." He began to gather his things.

"Shouldn't we hide the transport pods?" Erin asked.

"They would not know when they landed here. They are very old remember?" Tresodin answered.

Erin and Kamarin's eyes met as they gathered up their provisions for the trip. The incident of Kamarin's surprise attack was quickly forgotten.

In actuality the journey through the forest took all day and into the night.

When the foursome finally exited the cover of the trees, they again rested awhile as they waited to see the sunrise.

Slowly and beautifully, the dark night became dawn when the first sun shone itself above the horizon. Something lying in the valley beyond could barely be made out. It was not until the rise of the second sun however, when it was made light enough so they could finally see what was there. It lit up the city before them and it was wondrous. As the sun's rays glinted off the buildings, made of a bluish tinted marble, a marvelous hue of indigo shadowed the city.

Kamarin sat for a moment and imagined his people filling the streets coming to welcome him. But it was very quiet. The city was abandoned. The buildings were amassed in a skillful chain-like design stretching down through the valley. From where they stood they could not see the end of some of the homes along a large river's banks on which they had been assembled.

Such a beautiful city, everywhere flowers, and many vines had grown wild covering the lower halves of the buildings and streets.

Making their way to what appeared to be the city's center, a huge fountain of water shot up at least a hundred feet into the air and looked to be twenty-five more feet in diameter. From there the river flowed in opposite directions. Oddly, the river split the city in-two and there were no bridges. How could the two halves of the city function as one without bridges connecting them? But, more strangely, where was the water coming from?

Standing at the river's edge, Kamarin could wonder no longer.

"Tresodin! Where does this water come from?"

"Taste it," Tresodin replied.

"What for?"

"Just 'taste' it. It is not poisonous."

Kamarin stooped down, scooped a handful, sipped it, and then quickly spat it out. "It's salty!"

"Yes! You see, it comes from the Thelonan sea, the largest of our planet's oceans. It begins just on the other side of that mountain range. The water comes from there through an underground conduit. Because we are at a lower elevation, the pressure is enough to create the geyser you see here."

"But of what use it? Since it is salty- you cannot drink it," said Erin.

"Ah! But you see, under the city are miles of filters that are maintained by hundreds of robots. They assure the integrity of the drinking water supplied to the city. The rest is used to turn the city's turbines for unlimited power."

"How do we reach the other side of the city?" Kamarin questioned him as Erin tried to judge the distance to the other side.

"Curious-isn't it? Well, below the river is more of our city."

"But how?" asked Erin, taking it all in as if a child would.

"Well, under the river is a channel built above the city below it. The geyser you see is actually piped from further below."

"You mean you just walk under all of this water?" she asked.

"Precisely! That's all there is to it," Tresodin said.

"I would like to see it!" Erin exclaimed.

"There will be time enough later. But now I think we should find a place to hold up. Tresodin, where is the safest place?" asked Kamarin.

"Ahem! Well, under the city," he said.

It was important for them to quickly locate the communication center so they might find a way to contact other survivors of the Great war. Tresodin had described how many of them had taken refuge on distant planets, as did his parents. Now it was time for them to come home.

Before they found the entrance to the underground, they came upon a central city building with many steps. Tresodin explained how this was the first capital structure of this ancient city and where the council had conducted their business long ago. From here, they had directed the exploration of the ancient's new Thelona.

"This was the house of the people," Tresodin said proudly. "Inside is a recognizer. Activate it and it will send out a coded pulse beacon that only our people can recognize."

He was right. Just inside the huge entrance was a pedestal that they gathered around.

"Start it, Tresodin," Kamarin said, looking around on guard.

Tresodin laid his hand on the small electronic screen but nothing happened.

"I'm sorry, I cannot."

"What do you mean?" Kamarin asked frustratingly.

"Kamarin, it will only accept the hand print of a Guardian, no one will return unless a Guardian tells them to." he said as he humbly backed away.

As Kamarin stepped up to the recognizer, all of his friends stared. He knew that this was the final test. Was 'he' the Guardian? And when he did start the pulse beacon, it would begin a chain reaction through out the galaxy that could only be stopped with the annihilation of his enemies.

Kamarin slowly began to stand proud as he laid his hand upon the screen.

Then he looked through the glass sky-roof above them. "It is time for you to return and reclaim your home, 'oh great people' of Thelona!" Kamarin shed a tear wishing his mother and father could have been apart of it. But they would never see Thelona again.

"Seven"

The city slowly began to come to life again as power grids were switched back on, with the return of some of the lost children of Thelona.

Small bands of Gorin fighters, who had been patrolling Thelona's atmosphere, were quickly dispatched by Kamarin's new elite fighters, making it safe for all of his people who were returning.

His metal men stood guard every night at the city's gates to insure their safety while most were asleep.

In just a few days, the city was again alive with people. Most of the original inhabitants were older now but never too old for a fight. The major attack that would surely come when Voltar received word of the recall. Any soldiers or any Gorin equipment that had been left over from the Great war of his parents was silenced so that Voltar could not be warned. Kamarin knew that eventually Voltar would receive the same transmission that all other Thelonans were now receiving, but it was he himself that would have to hear the pulses emanating from the beacon. Pulses only recognizable by Thelonans. Kamarin could only hope that it would be a long time before Voltar could hear the message to return.

They would need as much time as they could get now to organize for the eminent attack. The Thelonans were still going to be overpowered by the new Gorin warships and the hologram-like titans they projected.

Some of Kamarin's people were returning with the rumor of at least six more spacecraft of this type that now existed. When Voltar eventually realizes that he had not destroyed Thelona, a huge blunder, he undoubtedly will be furious. It had been a blessing that he never revisited the annihilated planet to find that it was Skyberia and not Thelona he had destroyed. Even his own Gorin soldiers believed it to be Skyberia and had been stationed there permanently to keep an eye on any would be visitors to the burned out Thelona.

Kamarin now stood in front of a thousand original inhabitants of Thelona. Most of which had children with them. It was not near the number that he had hoped for, but the fact that they were brave enough to come back home made him proud.

Wherever they had taken refuge during the last twenty years, it was evident that they were still very strong in mind and body. The years indeed had been very kind to them.

Lort and Erin accompanied Kamarin up the long steps to the entrance of the council's building where he could address his people.

Tresodin turned to his people. "Some of you know who I am! And all of you know that you would not have been called home if a Guardian would not be present! Most of you remember Laith and Tessa Mitchel- two of our most beloved appointed Guardians. Well- you should know that they, for one reason or another, have long since passed away."

The crowd began to mumble to each other wondering why they were called back if there was no Guardian.

"I tell you now, they have not totally abandoned us! In fact, it is true to be the opposite! You see- born to the ancient blood of the Thelonan warrior- is Kamarin! Kamarin MITCHEL, Guardian of Orion and of our beloved Thelona!"

As Kamarin walked up to the pedestal, he gave Tresodin a look of insecurity, but the crowd roared cheering for him, all vowing loyalty to him.

"Loyalty to Kamarin! Delivered to us by the creator! Protector of all Orion!" they repeated.

"I am pleased that I am welcome by my people of Thelona! I realize that you do not know me but I am here to serve you and I will serve you well!"

The crowd cheered again, chanting. "Kamarin, child of Thelona Born of the Creator."

"You have all been in my heart since the time when I was young and my mother first revealed you to me. I have come to know my destiny is with you. There will be a day when Thelona will again be mother of Orion. But today is not that day. Before peace can be restored I will need your help. All of your skills will be greatly needed. I have not been to your underground city, but this is where we will have to live and work until we can again be free. Yes, we are home but it is not yet truly again 'ours'. Voltar still rules this galaxy and his armies must be stopped!

I know that you are not a warring people but your ancestral blood cries out! Before the Great war you had conquered many things. One of them being war. But now it is forced upon us again and we cannot ignore it. The old fighting ways of our ancestors will return to you, but in the end we will be even the wiser for it for 'peace' will be assured us once more. We will not flee this time! This time is ours. We will not run. This time we fight!" Kamarin raised his fist to the sky. And the people cheered.

"Now we must take refuge in the city below, we have so much to do!" Tresodin said as he began to lead the way.

"What will you have them do, Kamarin?" Erin asked.

"Some will be needed to begin research on more metal men. The others on new weaponry."

"But that will take too long."

"Perhaps- that is why Lort and I will start looking for the other metal men that have been hidden away all these years."

"You will not be able to acquire them without me," Erin said, feeling betrayed that he did not include her.

"I suppose you are right."

"So when do we leave?"

"Umm- I'll let you know," Kamarin said as he changed direction to help some of the people with their belongings and their children, to the underground entrance.

Robin L. Amrine

Erin had a funny feeling that he was avoiding her and was not telling her the truth, but she lent a hand too as they disappeared into the dark tunnel.

Several days had gone by and Kamarin was excited to see how well his people were readapting to this new situation. There was actually no disharmony among them at all. In fact, they all loved every minute of their newly assigned duties. All were ecstatic at having come home.

When Kamarin was satisfied they were all well settled in, he decided to recruit Tresodin's help again to locate the metal men of the dead Guardians. Kamarin had left his own metal men to stand guard at their city. Then he and the old scientist made their way down through the valley.

Their destination- was a place Tresodin called registry (#3). He had explained to Kamarin, that five of such places were built to store information. But before the war, they had been modified. Turned into vaults to contain the location of each families intended location. And only a Guardian would have access to the information stored there.

The trouble with Tresodin's plan was that he was not sure how the vaults were protected. He only knew of their location. It was possible that one or even all three of the metal men could be found there.

Kamarin had no way to know how much time he had before Voltar would attack Thelona, so with every step his pace quickened.

The two of them- having sneaked away from the city walked for days, until at the edge of a newly found forest, Treosodin paused at the trailhead into it.

-*-

The entrance signal went off again- and again- as Voltar tried to stretch himself to reach the door's remote control; the entrance to his living quarters. He had to really stretch from his seat of his machine of life.

"Come in! Come in! Can't anyone hear anymore?" Voltar said as he sat back in his reclined seat after conquering the entrance button.

"Hello, great master!" Ogel said, bouncing into the room.

"Don't great master me! I am no one's master. Not since another sits in my place of power," Voltar grumbled.

"Going anywhere tonight? Looks like there's only room for one on that machine of yours master." Ogel said as he grabbed a piece of fruit and jumped into another chair. Making himself comfortable he stopped chewing for a moment and smiled a quirky smile at his commander.

Thinking he would not have to put up with him too much longer, Voltar tried to ignore his impudence. "Is it done?" he asked.

"You can't expect me to just barge into his room and kill him straight away?"

"Why not? You seem to have little regard in your attitude with me—your master."

"Oh, sorry about that," Ogel said swinging a dangled foot over the arm of the chair and biting again into the stolen fruit.

As the time counter on Voltar's machine started to come- up all zeros, a green light came on to show him he could now disconnect.

His lifeline hissed as he unhooked, and during the process Ogel jumped to his feet to watch.

"You know that's really something. I always wondered how you did that."

"Want to try it?" Voltar asked him, holding up the hose end.

"Hugh? Well, I don't think I'll be needing something like that for quite some time."

"Oh—you never know," Voltar said with a snicker. Ogel stopped chewing to see the expression on his face, trying to understand the implication.

Voltar was full of anxiety. He was dealing with the fact that he was no longer young and was much less powerful than Ogel. Especially when he was not in control of the powerful Gorin army. The slime dog that took his place in his absence had also taken from him, credit due him. He, without a doubt, had to be dealt with, one way or another.

If this fellow traitor to Thelona must be killed, who now sat on Voltar's thrown, then it would have to be soon.

The next attacks, the Gorin were to make, would be directed to the outer Rotterahm planets, these were the first of many worlds helped by the Thelonans before the 'great' war. They had been outfitted to defend the Orion system from any outside hostile people. It was a kind of task Thelona had really just intended as a gesture to help restore the outer planet's economy. They really were not prepared for anything they might unleash on them. They would have never suspected an attack would come from inside the galaxy, anyway. Once they are able to get through this fortified perimeter, the only formidable force that threatened to keep the Gorin from their conquest, they would be free to dominate other worlds in many other galaxies! And with them the wealth and popularity would be given to their leader. Voltar was determined even more that their leader would indeed be 'him'.

At his age he was not into the physical aspect of domination and the pleasures the booty might bring. He only required the importance of ownership, OK, and some of the treasures. His slightly less powerful position allowed him to devise a plan of assassination, if Ogel would not be his pawn and help murder the Gorin leader- there were many who would.

"Do you have a plan to kill him? I assume you do because you definitely act as if you have everything under control," Voltar said.

"Don't worry. You'll be in full control very soon." Ogel said with a mouthful- chewing disgustingly provoking.

"That is good you have a plan because you have just twenty-one days! At that time we will attack the Rotterahm. By then you better have taken care of business. I and I alone, will lead the armada against them. If you want to be a part of it, you'll do the job you've been paid for or forfeit everything. And I do mean everything!"

Ogel might usually act irrationally, but he was not stupid. He knew what he was getting at. He also knew he could not yet show his hand for his true intentions, even though Voltar was trying him so. The best thing for him now, would be to do as Voltar wished- until he could make his move against him. He was fearful of Voltar's men who were always on guard outside in the hall. They would surely kill him if he tried anything now.

"Is that a threat?" he asked Voltar with a grin.

"My dear young friend, I never make threats- only promises!"

"Voltar opened the door for Ogel to leave and tauntingly winked.

"You kill me Voltar, you'll never find Kamarin Mitchel without me."

"He is dead! You know that!" Voltar said angrily.

"Oh yes, I forgot. Where did you say you buried the body?" Ogel winked back, did an about face, and marched down the long hall in a mocking gesture.

"Imbecile." Voltar mumbled, and then slammed the door closed behind him.

Looking out of his apartment window, Voltar could see his rival with his you friends, a select few protecting him as he made his way through the crowds below.

He wondered if Ogel was right. Was Kamarin Mitchel still alive? Not that it could even matter now. But if he was, Voltar knew he would loose any respect the Gorin people might still have for him.

He often wondered if he had made the right decision in assuming Kamarin was dead. If, it was- a mistake, then this, too would have to be rectified. Deep down, he knew he would have to.

"Eight"

Tresodin stopped in front of Kamarin abruptly, as they topped a hill overlooking a small clearing in a heavily wooded area.

"There it is!" he whispered, pointing to a large pole in the center of the clearing.

Curious, Kamarin began to walk towards the clearing but the old man held him back by the arm and whispered again.

"I wouldn't," he said, motioning to him to hide in some nearby brush.

"Why are you hesitating?" asked Kamarin.

"I gave it a lot of thought as to how my fellow scientists might have protected the registries and I have come to a disturbing conclusion."

"What are you talking about?" Kamarin was now showing his impatience.

"Watch!" he said as he picked up a stone and threw it into the clearing.

Without a sound, a large and very strange cat-like creature suddenly appeared as if from out of no where, from behind the pole. It seemed to be attached to the pole by a large chain draped from his throat.

Kamarin could not believe what he was seeing. The creature was much too large to have been hiding behind the pole.

"Where did it come from?" he asked.

"I knew it! Gillman must have succeeded."

"What?"

"Albert Gillman, my closest friend and colleague. He found a key to unlock the door!"

"The wha…?"

"The door, my boy! The door to the other world! The dimension where this 'beast' has just come from."

"Hugh? Th….this is too much for me, old man, just what are we supposed to do now?" Kamarin asked as he breathed faster, clutching the handle of his long knife.

"That will not help us. If his chain had been any longer, we both would be dead now. We should have invited your friends to come with us."

"And why is that? So that they might be eaten along with us?"

"By all means, no! Its just that Erin could calm the beast long enough for us to retrieve the information we are looking for."

"Calm 'that' thing? You've 'got' to be kidding."

Just then something tapped Kamarin on his shoulder and startled him so that he fell back into the bushes, ready for a fight.

He then realized that it was Erin and Lort. They had managed to sneak up on them. Under different circumstances, that would have been difficult.

Erin started to giggle and suddenly drove her machine past him into the clearing.

"No, Erin, come back!" Kamarin began loosing control of the situation, when he realized Erin was too close and was now in reach of the beast's chain.

"Oh, no! It's too late for me now!" she said as she continued for the beast, with her hands raised giggling.

But the beast from the other world or wherever it came from, did not attack. Instead, it began to purr, arch it's back and snap its tail from side to side.

The ground rumbled as the giant feline lay down next to her while she vigorously scratched its chin.

"I don't understand. The giant beast is greeting her." Kamarin said, still- a little shaken.

"There was little time to explain. Erin's family, were from the hidden valley here on Thelona. In that valley, her people lived with these wild animals. Neither of them would ever harm the other." Tresodin said, with a smile.

Kamarin looked at Erin picturing her on Thelona a long time ago. Even though she had never been there, it was like she never left. Her people truly were a part of this world.

"Well, you tried to leave without me, and I told you that you would never find the other metal men without me, didn't I?" she asked Kamarin.

Kamarin was speechless and began to slowly walk around her and her strange feline friend. But as he passed the large cat, it swiftly moved it's gigantic paw in front of him and started to wrap it around his legs.

Kamarin froze and called to Erin with a whisper. "Ugh- now what?" The big cat eyed him closely.

"Don't worry, he just likes you, Kamarin." Erin rubbed its cheek and the big cat closed his eyes releasing his grip to move closer to her. That giant cat's head alone dwarfed her.

Kamarin moved slowly towards the pole where the beast had appeared.

Then- turning again to check on his friends, they had vanished! Or was it he that had left them behind? Could he really have gone to another world like Tresodin said? The huge cat had to have come from somewhere and it seemed this was the beast's place of origin. He felt as if he was surrounded by a void.

Thelona had completely disappeared from his sight, and now before him, was a table of stone.

He noticed it was some kind of room that he was now standing in.

Doorways began to open ahead of him, and to the side. Then three intense bright lights came towards him. They were so powerful he could not keep his eyes open. The only sounds he could hear were of three loud heart-beats, they were coming closer.

Something was put into his hand by an unknown- he could not see. Then the lights went out.

When Kamarin opened his eyes he found himself with his friends again.

He quickly realized that that was yet another adventure, for yet another time.

"I'm back!" he said, feeling him-self to be sure.

"What do you mean? You did not go anywhere. You've been standing there all the while," Erin said, still stroking the cat beast.

Kamarin smiled and looked down at his hand, he then was reassured he was not imagining things.

"Then what is this?" he asked, holding up the object.

All eyes were poised upon it. It was a short staff with the face of a lion carved in its handle.

"It is a memory staff!" Tresodin said excitedly. "Who ever holds it and keeps it in his possession will have all events recorded into it.

"What should I do with it?" asked Kamarin.

"You see the sharp end there? Stick that end in the ground."

Kamarin did as Tresodin instructed.

They gathered around to see what might happen.

Erin set the big cat free form his chain and he lumbered off into the woods.

"What's it doing?" Erin asked.

Tresodin shushed her to be quiet.

The strange artifact began to vibrate in the ground, and a rainbow of lights sprang from its top, dancing above their heads.

The streams of light converged back to the center and then a figure of a man appeared.

"Who are you?" Kamarin asked the apparition.

"I am the image of Malcome Paladees!"

"He was one of the chosen ones," Tresodin whispered to Kamarin.

"You summoned me here?"

"We...I guess I did. Where did you hide your metal man, Paladees?" Kamarin asked.

"I am afraid I cannot answer that question."

"Why can't you, Paladees?" Tresodin asked.

"I do not know who you are and I have been instructed to hold this secret very dear."

"I am Kamarin Mitchel, son of Laith and Tessa Mitchel, the last of the Guardians of Orion. They are dead and I have survived them. Is this information good enough for you?"

"Yes, it seems to suffice. Actually my program for this subject was to allow only fellow Guardians to access this information, but I believe- the second generation Guardian should be allowed."

"Now listen closely to my question, image of Malcome Paladees, because we are in a great hurry. Where is your metal man?" Kamarin grew tired of trying to communicate with a computer image, but felt he had little choice.

"The metal man is called 'Artamous'. He is the one you seek. You may find him in the wind tunnels of Shinnaroo. There in the depths, I have hidden him."

Without hesitation Kamarin grabbed the staff, pulling it from the ground. The projected image of the late Guardian disappeared.

"Which way do we go, Tresodin?" he asked.

Tresodin turned and started back down the same trail they used to find the clearing.

This time Erin and her friend Lort followed close behind.

"Kamarin! What if we meet up with the Gorin? You left your metal men back at the city." asked Erin.

Kamarin did not answer her. Instead he took large fast paces to exit the forest He knew that they were vulnerable now but he felt they had no time to waste. They would just have to avoid any contact with their enemy until their task was completed.

Reaching the edge of the forest and its protective canopy, Kamarin stopped when a feeling came over him. A peculiar one- he had not had before. It was as if something or someone was trying to persuade him to go in a different direction. He felt compelled to go 'back' into the clearing in the woods. He fought the urge and went on. His sights were set on retrieving the metal men and nothing else.

"Where is Shinaroo, Tresodin?" Kamarin asked.

"The tunnels of Shinaroo are in the cliffs at the river's delta. We are not far from there now. We should be there before nightfall."

-*-

Kamarin could hear the surf crashing against the rocks far below the cliffs where they stood. He could barely make out the caves on the adjacent cliff wall for it was quite dark now. They would have reached them earlier if it had not been for Erin's machine breaking down. Tresodin swore that when they returned to the city- he was going to take care of her problem. He continually commented about how old and worn the mechanical parts were and promised he would change things for her.

For now, they would make camp and investigate the tunnels in the morning. It was too dangerous in the dark for the tunnels had been carved out of the rocky cliffs by the wind and sea for centuries. Similar to a beehive, there were many entrances. The mouths of each cave were dangerously smooth, and the wind played through them as if they were musical

141

instruments creating beautiful sounds. Tonight the songs they played were very soothing.

Sleep came upon the group rather quickly.

Kamarin was very tired and drifted off into a deep sleep. He dreamt of his life when he was young on L-2. About the time his father died and when his mother gave him the metal men.

He then began to remember the times although short he had with his father. They were very different than those he spent with his mother. His father treated him always like a young man, and not as a child. He loved his father very much. He had always treated Kamarin with great love and respect. He recalled trying to be like his father, strong but gentle, inventive and very generously courageous. The lessons of survival his father was so adamant in teaching him had saved his life once. The greatest gift his father gave him however was the gift of caring. As when the earth moved and caused giant fishers in the mountains south of their colony, many people who lived there cried out for help. His father, with help from others from the surrounding colonies, without tools dug the survivors from the village's rubble, and he would not stop though his hands bled.

Kamarin tossed and turned in the night for he had not thought of his father since he and his mother had been banished from the colony. Why did he now?

He tried to hold onto his father's image for as long as he could but someone was trying to wake him. Kamarin wished whoever it was would go away so he could finish his dream. But reality won- and his eyes cracked open letting in the morning light.

"Good morning," he greeted Erin, as he sat up. "I trust you had a good night's sleep?"

"Yes. And I trust you did, too?"

"Trust me, I didn't. It was interesting, though." he said, rubbing his eyes with his open palms.

"What was so interesting?" she asked, her brows lowered with concern.

"Don't you listen to any of your dreams?"

"I don't have dreams."

"Do you have any secret hopes or wishes?"

"Oh yes! But I don't dream." she shook her head.

"You have dreams- you just don't remember them."

"I remember my hopes and my wishes."

"What do you wish for?" Kamarin asked, but Erin suddenly could not speak, having quickly become unusually shy and turning her head away.

"What's wrong, Erin?"

Tresodin interrupted, "Kamarin! We must hurry, the tide is out, and the water is below all of the tunnels. I estimate we have an hour before it returns".

'SAVED', Erin thought.

Kamarin's concern for Erin grew more each day. He was afraid that she might become badly hurt and he would not be able to live with it. Their crusades seemed to be getting more dangerous every time. He felt this was no place for a woman in her condition, but he would not be able to convince her to stay behind, DEFINITLEY NOT Erin. She probably is the most headstrong woman he had ever met. And quite possibly the prettiest.

The only way they had to reach one of the tunnels was for someone to be lowered on a rope, since there were no trees or rocks for an anchor, 'Lort' would have to do.

There were many tunnels of different sizes that were formed into the cliffs. Kamarin had no idea which one he should explore first.

With Lort holding fast to the rope, as anchor, Kamarin kicked off of the edge.

Repelling at least sixty feet down, he had checked out several shallow holes and was swinging from to the side trying to investigate a larger far deeper hole, when a blast of air from it, sent him out and away from the cliff's face. He bobbed and swayed from the wind tunnel's effect and it seemed impossible to get back to the rock's face.

Kicking hard, trying to escape the force of the wind, he covered his face while trying to breathe.

It was then- he suddenly felt a slamming sting to his shoulder.

Rolling to the side in the air-stream, he could see his attacker.

There, hovering approximately a hundred yards away, was a Gorin patrol fighter.

It fired again with only a near miss.

Lort, realizing Kamarin could not move to avoid being hit again- pulled on the rope which only caused him to bob up and down in the blasts of air from the giant sea cave.

The Gorin fighter would not come any closer, trying hard to stay clear of the wind tunnel's turbulence, It's operator undoubtedly could see that Kamarin was trapped and moved to fire upon his anchor- Lort. Of course, Lort could not move or he would loose Kamarin at the other end.

The enemy was only toying with them now. The fighter fired at Lort but just knocked some of the cliff away from under his footing.

Lort was enraged at being so helpless.

As the others took aim and fired at the fighter, it quickly lowered again to Kamarin's position.

Another blast clipped him in the leg this time. Kamarin knew that the pilot of the craft had nothing better to do and would torture him with disabling shots until he was ripped to pieces.

He struggled with the wind again but to no avail.

Then with one mighty pull- Lort was able to snap Kamarin to the top of the cliff and out of harms way. Within seconds of each other's actions, a giant hand came suddenly from out of nowhere, and swatted the Gorin fighter to the rocky cliff wall. As it blew up in a huge ball of flames it fell burning into the ocean below. Kamarin looked up to see a metal man hovering where the Gorin fighter had been.

"Look!" Erin said. "Where did it come from and how did it know we were in trouble?"

Kamarin bedded down on the ground and he remembered what his mother had told him about the metal men. "They will come when they know you are in danger," But this was not one of Kamarin's metal men. This was a new and different metal man. "It must be the one that had been hidden fore so long in the tunnels," he said. It had come to life to save them.

"Now you have two that can fly, Kamarin." Erin said as they all came to the realization that their family had just grown.

One down, Kamarin thought, as he relaxed at the top of the cliff overlooking the ocean.

"Nine"

Erin persistently tried to convince Kamarin to return with them to the city, she was very concerned about his shoulder, but Kamarin insisted that he would be all right. He did admit that the wound in his leg hurt a bit, but that they were not very serious and were not bleeding. The heat from the laser blast had seared them closed.

Kamarin directed them to return home without him and wait. He told them he had some unfinished business to attend to and that he would rejoin them soon.

But Erin had bad feelings whenever they were separated. She felt something was bothering him so she agreed to go on ahead on the condition that he would take the newly found metal man with him, and he agreed.

Kamarin was somehow being drawn again to the place in the woods where they had found the memory staff.

The clearing was empty now and the beast that was once protecting the door was long gone.

As he searched for the opening to the other side, he felt especially alone. This time, he could not find the opening to the other world. Where did it go he thought as he spread out his arms to see if he could touch it, but there was nothing, the calling he had felt was even stronger now, but why?

Suddenly deciding that there were many things he could not understand and this was one of them, he turned to leave.

Just then he was startled. In front of him was a ghostly figure of a man. It was his father!

Kamarin looked around for another memory staff projecting the image, but there wasn't one.

"Kamarin, my son!"

Kamarin could not reply he was so shocked.

"Kamarin, there are things you must know about the Gorin," the apparition told him.

"Are you my father or just his memory?" Kamarin asked- his voice cracked until it was fully audible.

"I am but a memory."

This could be some kind of trick, Kamarin thought.

"Then where is the memory stick?"

"My image has come across time to warn you."

"Where is this place you come from and what do you wish to tell me?"

"The source of my projection is not important. What 'is' important- is for you to understand fully who and what you are up against."

"Go on," Kamarin said while thinking how much he had sorely missed his father and his mother. As he listened to his father's image give detailed descriptions of the Gorin strengths and weaknesses, his heart once again ached for their company.

Kamarin had already found out about most of what the recording was trying to warn him of, but some of the information would be very helpful.

"Is that all?" Kamarin asked the apparition.

"No, not quite, Kamarin. If the Gorin fully implement the use of the holograms, it could be too late to stop them."

"Hugh?" Kamarin wondered how an old recording of his father could have updated information about the Gorin?

Then came a final jolt to his soul.

"Kamarin, it is wonderful to see you again. Your mother was right. I am very proud of you!" The image suddenly faded away into nothingness.

"Wait!" Kamarin yelled. All this time he had somehow been communicating with his father. He believed the image to be another recording- but it was his 'father', but how?

Kamarin smiled and an elated feeling of strength filled his body. They are Guardians, he thought, they have been and always would be in his life.

Kamarin no longer felt the pain from his wounds as he made his way back to the city, at least he gave them no attention.

As he found one of the secret doorways to the under river city, he noticed that on the surface it was absolutely quiet. This was good it was exactly how he expected to find it. He had told his people to take refuge underground until he returned. The major portion of the ancient city that was under the river was at least three hundred feet below. Several miles of interconnecting ramp-style tunnels such as the he was in formed many secret entrances they all finally converged into one massive hangar bay type area at the heart of the city.

In the tunnel he was in, many of his people were running around rummaging through containers of ship supplies. This scene resembled a happy traders' bizarre. This was good. Supplies were plenty but if they were to go to war now, everything would have to happen sequentially in their favor to be lucky enough to defeat the Gorin.

The power of the Gorin was a very frightening thing to most of the inhabitants of Orion, and with their new weapon, Kamarin knew that only three, of the original five metal men, still might not be enough to balance the scale. The fight, if it were to take place now, could be long and too many of his people could die as a result. It was a chance he could not afford to take, considering their welfare first and foremost.

Kamarin was not yet familiar with the outer planetary forces and their strengths. However, they happened to be the only fighting force even remotely capable of fending off the Gorin. This was but an irritation to the mighty Voltar and by no means was he intimidated by their feeble force; comparing it to his own. The only reason they had not yet been targeted was that he wanted to control the inner regions of the galaxy first and then hunt for Kamarin and his friends. There would be a slight disadvantage now for the Gorin to attack the outer planets' defenses and it was the time it would take for them to engage all of them with a large enough force. They would have plenty of time to prepare for an attack later even though it would be futile for these planets to try to defend themselves. Surprise had been Voltar's greatest ally- until now. For now he had the ultimate weapon and it was as easy as turning on a switch. And through a beam of light, he now had metal men of his own, yet still- they may not be as powerful as Kamarin's metal men.

Even though the Gorin possessed this great power, Kamarin knew also they harbored a weakness. The ships that created the hologram images also controlled their every move. The Thelonans knew that the warships would have to be their main targets, for their ships had there own inherent weaknesses, but how were they going to use this to their advantage to destroy them? And when would the opportunity present itself? Only time would tell.

So far Kamarin was only able to locate one of the metal men he was searching for. It was a small miracle in itself to have found him. He still would have to find the others. Tresodin knew nothing more that could help him locate them, and Erin still claimed to be his ticket in retrieving them. Could she really help him? All of these questions made him very tired, and as he watched his people busy at work, he fell asleep in a pile of winter clothing. Stacked in the aisle, broken loose from a large shipping bale, he rested in the middle of them.

He began to dream again, and again, it was of things in his past. Mostly of his parents before his father had died. He remembered how happy they once were long ago on L-2.

Stirring as he slept, the years flashed before him. It pleased him to relive some events and frustrated him to confront those that were not so pleasurable. He smiled as he remembered his mother. The wind in her hair and long flowing dress made her beauty burn bright in his memory of her. Oddly, a memory came to him that he did not remember. His mother stood on a hill, her dress gently flowing in the wind as she pointing to a small moon, but it was no ordinary moon. This moon was attached to the planet on which she stood, by some sort of bridge stretched between them. Surely he could create ANYTHING in his dreams, he thought as he shook his head in his sleep, a foot-bridge between two planets? Unbelievable! Not possible! Who would have built it?

Kamarin quietly chuckled in his sleep while Erin gently shook him to wake him.

"Boy, are we glad to see you," she said, turning her machine to get a more comfortable look at him.

"What is it?" Kamarin asked yawning, and stretching.

"They're going to attack!" said Erin.

"What do you mean? Where?" Kamarin sat erect.

"I can only tell you that it is not here, and it is not now, but if we don't stop them we will loose it all!"

"Please, Erin, don't play games with me! Tell me-what you are talking about?"

"We received word that the outer united forces are under attack. It is believed to be only a preemptive strike and that a larger one is expected."

"I know nothing of the outer forces capabilities. I'm not sure what to do."

"And they don't know about you yet either."

151

"Well, who are they, Erin?" asked Kamarin.

"They are a feeble fighting force made up of all the outer planetary systems of Orion. Unfortunately for them they are the only army that now stands between Voltar and free space, other galaxies will fall victim to the Gorin. We have to help them defeat the Gorin, Kamarin." Erin's hand shook as she grasped his.

"First things first, Erin, where is Tresodin?"

"I don't know, why? What do you want with him?"

"I have to ask him about a bridge."

"The sky bridge? To the sand moon Bandagoon?" Erin asked.

"You know of it?"

"Everyone does."

"Take me there!" Kamarin motioned for her to lead the way.

"It will take several days and we will need some provisions and some protective wear. It is very windy on Bandagoon and because of the sand, it is brutal and visibility is quite low, almost like Tresodin's barrier he created at his home. I personally have not been there yet but my mother told me all about that place. Many travelers go there in search of recreation. Many different life forms travel to that place…It will be most interesting to visit there."

Erin continued to show her excitement as she rambled and they walked down an adjoining tunnel, while Kamarin searched for Lort.

Lort was busily entertaining some of the children in one of the city's underground courtyards.

The children were pretending to be stronger than him and he allowed them to easily knock him to the ground and tie him up.

A small four-year old girl had a very dangerous case of the 'giggles' and anxiously waited for her chance.

As Erin and Kamarin came into the play area, Lort spotted them and started to sit upright, but the little girl took this as an opportunity and leaped to his chest. Luckily, both Erin and Kamarin were just able to witness the little girl land one square on Lort's big nose, and the granite man was down again.

The little girl let out a big laugh. Suddenly she reared back and let him have it again.

Lort's eyes began to water.

"Need a hand, big fella?" Kamarin asked, reaching out to give him his hand. Lort just smiled through the tears.

"Met your match finally, Hugh?" Erin asked, giggling.

"It is not the first time- you were also young once," Lort said as he picked the little girl gently from him and sent her on her way. "Are we leaving again for somewhere?" he picked himself up and sniffed a bit.

"Yep!" Erin said, grabbing hold of his large hand to lead him out of the park.

With having gathered their things and enough provisions for their trip, they stood at the city's gate and made last minute preparations to leave.

The old scientist, Tresodin, gave them each a pair of goggles for the sandy winds they would encounter on Bandagoon. One pair he had made special for Lort.

Then he sent them on their way bidding them farewell.

Kamarin took Deke with them and left the other two of his metal men to protect his people and their city.

-*-

The trail was not really hard to walk; but with their new air belts, traveling was even more of a breeze, floating above, and the sometimes-rocky path.

Erin's belt had been modified and fitted to her treader allowing her the same freedom as her two friends, although her controls were somewhat touchy, she felt top heavy.

The scenery Thelona had to offer along the way was breathtaking. Rolling hills of grass with groves of trees resembling orchards were as far as they could see. Many different shades of greens and even some blue stood out from all the different browns. Flowers seemed to have been purposely placed by the Thelonans who had once cared for the land. Many small mammals and birds could be approached easily because of the quiet whisper of their air belt's engines. To think that this world was supposed to have been destroyed was quite upsetting, however Thelona was not yet out of danger.

Lort never had it so good, not having to walk on his own big feet this time around. The warm breeze on his face and gentle up and down motion of his flight was beginning to put him to sleep.

As his eyes clamped shut, he accidentally collided with Kamarin in mid-air, sending Kamarin into a nearby tree.

Fully awake now, he gasped as he watched his friend tumble down the full length of the tree. The limbs, quite large and full of needle growth, affectedly slowed the speed of Kamarin's fall before he hit the ground in a daze.

Lort flew to Kamarin's side- afraid he might have really hurt him.

"What happened?" Kamarin asked, trying to stop his head from spinning.

"I am sorry, Guardian! I guess I must have bumped into you." Lort sorely admitted.

"On purpose you mean," said Kamarin.

"No! No! Absolutely not!' Lort was flabbergasted.

"Oh sure! Just thought you'd sneak in a shot when I had my back turned, eh?" Kamarin played on Lort's apologetic nature.

"No Guardian, wha...I mean, Kamarin sir, I mean, I would not have done that on purpose. I would never do anything of the sort!" he insisted.

"Well. I suppose you've been wanting to show me who's a better fighter from the 'beginning so I'll give you that one." Kamarin winked at Erin.

She just looked back at Kamarin and lowered her eyebrows.

"But! But!" Lort could not seem to explain fast enough.

"No, no, no, that's all right! At least I can still feel my legs," Kamarin said as he activated his air belt and again took to the air.

Lort looked at Erin and shrugged his broad shoulders as they again followed.

"That's all right Lort," Erin said, "You might have done him some good with a good jar like that."

155

Lort just shook his head from side to side in a state of confusion as he floated along.

Another few miles went by and Lort now serenely started to sway again ahead of Kamarin.

It wasn't long and Lort began to weave back and forth over the trail.

Kamarin closed the gap between them and waited for his chance.

Then Lort suddenly began to snore.

"That's it!" Kamarin said and leaped on Lort's back and started for another nearby tree, with Lort in tow.

Lort woke in a panic and stopped both of them just short of the tree. Grabbing his assailant, Lort threw him from his back and into the tree branches- again. His eyes suddenly got big in disbelief, It was too late. When he recognized it was Kamarin, he was bouncing again down another tree from branch to branch. Lort dove in trying to save him.

"What in the world are you two doing?" Erin yelled.

"Ooh! Ah! Oh! Ouch! Rats!" was all that could be heard coming from inside the tree branches as they shook violently.

Then- thud! Kamarin hit the ground again.

Lort floated out and hovered over the trail. "Not again." he said hopelessly. "Are you all right Guardian?" Lort asked.

"All right you…," Kamarin said suddenly, attacking Lort from the ground this time. He just pulled at his big feet trying to pluck him from the sky.

At this point Erin began to laugh.

Lort was still pretty confused and was trying to figure out why Kamarin was acting so strange. Then he saw Kamarin smile.

"OK, big Buddy!" Kamarin said as he took to flight and then slammed into Lort, grabbing his head trying to get a good hold.

For the next twenty to thirty minutes, Erin sat under a shade tree being entertained, as Kamarin was loosing terribly.

-*-

Bandagoon, a small moon not originally one of Thelona's, was yet another attraction left over from its earlier history. Legend was that it was a gift from the heavens making it a chosen planet from all the rest of Orion. Actual writings of the time, when it became a fixed satellite- close above Thelona's surface, recorded it as once being a part of a neighboring galaxy. In that galaxy it was found that two large planets had fallen out of their sun's orbit and collided with each other sending debris into their galaxy.

Because Bandagoon was made up primarily of an iron ore and Thelona's magnetic field was concentrated over a large deposit of the same, it had become trapped in one location over the planet's surface forever; truly a wondrous sight.

A gravity bridge had been built by the ancients to enable visitors to explore the sandy moon, with many small outposts to provide entertainment as means to refresh one's self. Bandagoon had shortly become well known in the galaxy. However slowly after the Gorin attack, it was a place few dared at times to visit because of the occasional passing of pirates.

The gravity bridge made a slow assent through the high clouds above them. It was then a straight shot to the moon. Standing at the entrance of the space walkway and following it up with ones eyes, there was a dizzy feeling of falling. Except it was not possible because the bridge had its own gravity and atmosphere. Yet it was not enclosed. Still for the gravity to have its effect, they would have to keep in contact with it at all times. The air belts would be of no use to them now.

None of them talked much as they took in the breathtaking beauty of Thelona while walking above the clouds. The trip being several miles would take them into the night and they would have to stay at one of the way stations the builders had provided, at every milepost, was a small covered cubicle to allow tourists to rest before continuing on.

As they lay down for the night, Erin showed no signs of being tired. She therefore seemed intent on keeping Kamarin awake, too.

"Kamarin, what will you do after you've defeated Voltar?" she asked whispering.

"I have not thought about it. Why?"

"Oh, I'm just curious. Do you plan to stay here on Thelona?"

"I will have to. I am the people's Guardian now. It is what I was born to do. I will have to protect them until another can replace me."

"Who will that be?" she asked.

"I don't really know, perhaps one of my children. Tell me- what will 'you' do?"

"Children, Hugh? One of your children," she said quietly to herself. "Well, I guess I will not have to protect Lort after we are through, but still, wherever he will go I will go also."

"You will protect Lort, Hugh?"

"Yes, I will protect him. Do you think I am incapable?"

"No, I do not. If anyone can, you would be the one."

"Thank you, I think. Why do you say, I can, of all people?"

"Well- ugh, you are beautifully intelligent and wonderfully valiant!"

"Beautiful? Are you saying that you think I am beautiful?"

"Ugh...I, ugh...you, hum...you look, I mean...we should go to sleep no, we have to start out again early." Kamarin was nervous about the direction the conversation was heading.

"No. Kamarin, what did you mean?" she insisted.

"I mean that I think- that you are very attractive. Now, I am tired and I have to go to sleep, OK?"

"Why sure you can, Kamarin. Please do not let me stop you," Erin said, smiling triumphantly.

Kamarin turned red and tried to conceal his head in his arms as if he were more interested in getting to sleep than he might be in her.

"Good night, Lort," Erin said.

"Good night, missy," he answered.

"Good night, Kamarin." She waited for his reply.

"Good night," he grumbled as he turned over to sleep but mainly to keep from facing her again.

Erin smiled while she stared into the starry night sky through a small porthole formed into the wall of the sleep station. She was happy, but she was also sad. At times like these she would forget that she was born without legs, but then again she knew she would never have them either. She felt that Kamarin cared for her, but why? With all that she wanted to offer him she felt she had little to give. And soon the machine that had literally been apart of her was certain to quit functioning. Then what would she do? She could not expect to be carried. Even though Lort would do such a thing, and what of Kamarin? A Guardian could never be tied to an invalid.

She soon destroyed her own happiness. The stars blurred in the sky as her tears began to fall. Silently she wept. She realized that it was more than revenge she was looking for. She wanted to be whole. Still, she refused to be denied her destiny, although her feelings could keep her from her own happiness and ultimately Kamarin.

Lighted walkways with safety cables for lifeline attachments, were the only safe ways to get around on Bandagoon. The continuous sand-storm was so thick, that it almost blocked out the light, from Thelona's largest sun. Without protective gear, anyone of them could become separated from the others and easily lost. They brought with them, heavy hooded-furs and their full faced goggles to stop the small sand particles from blasting the skin from their bones. Even Lort, having his own fur, preferred using one of another beast's to spare his own from the burning effect the tiny sand particles would have on his own hide.

With their vision- so impaired, it really did not surprise Kamarin when he rammed his head into what felt like a rock wall.

"I found a wall!" he yelled behind to the others.

"How do you know it is a wall?" Lort asked.

"Because it sounded hollow when I hit it with my head!"

"Are you sure it was the wall?" Erin laughed.

Suddenly a bright light covered them as a door cracked open in the wall, and a dark figure waved to them to enter.

"Come in! Come in! Welcome! Welcome," the stranger said as he helped them in, fighting the wind to close the door behind them.

Inside, a large man stood in front of Kamarin while two others had their weapons drawn and trained on Lort and Erin.

Kamarin swiftly and instinctively grabbed the man in front of him by the throat and slammed him against the wall holding him high so that his feet could not touch the ground.

At the same time- Lort swung his huge arm knocking the other two into the crowded bar. 'Good night!" he said knowing they would not be getting up soon.

Before the bulky man's voice box was crushed, he squeaked out, "Who are you?" Someone in the crowd yelled, "He is the GUARDIAN!"

Feeling that the man meant no more threat to him or anyone else, Kamarin loosened his grip.

"Why did you attack us?" asked Kamarin sternly.

"We were just checking you 'out'. You can't be too careful in a place like this, you know."

"You don't say," said Kamarin.

"Yes. There have been many raiders in this galaxy and we have made it a habit to make everyone's business 'our' business."

"Well, it's 'none' of your business," Kamarin told the big man, releasing him, then made his way through to the bar.

"Guardian, May I suggest that we have our refreshments and leave. This is not the safest place to be it appears," Lort said quietly so as not to give up any control of the situation. He was very much on guard now and caught a man looking at them a little longer than he was comfortable with and decided suddenly that the man needed a nap. SLAM! Lort slapped the man's head to the bar, and he went down limp as a rag.

"I'll take it into consideration, big fella," said Kamarin. "Lort, that's enough."

Kamarin happened to notice two dark figures leave through a back entrance when the three of them approached the bar. He wanted to follow but Lort needed comforting. Otherwise he might clean out the whole place. Besides, Kamarin knew that it would be nearly impossible to chase them in the sandstorm.

"Gorin soldiers just left out the back," he whispered to his friends.

"Do you want me to get them for you?" asked Lort, always faithful.

"No, that's all right, but you can bet that they're running back to tell their boss about us."

"If you want, I will hunt them down," Lort offered, again holding up his hammer.

"Let them go. It's better for us to get it over sooner than later anyway. Besides we have more pressing matters."

"I don't like it here, Kamarin," Erin said, looking around moving closer to Lort.

"I just need a little information and then we'll go," Kamarin said, trying to calm her.

Kamarin knew that with their dramatic entrance they definitely had everyone's attention, but he needed information and no one was too likely now to freely offer him any.

"Who is the proprietor of this establishment?" he asked the man tending bar.

"He is dead. Hee! Hee!" the man said as laughter erupted throughout the place.

"And who took his life- you?" Kamarin asked, assuming from their reaction that that was what had happened.

"Oh- no! He in fact took it himself!"

Then another suddenly spoke. "Yeah! The old rooster crowed his last- right before he passed out stone cold there on the bar!"

The crowd could not keep from laughing from the men's comments. "He still had the stench of liquor when he was laying out back until the sand worms had their fill. Yep! Some pretty happy worms they turned out to be! Hee! Hee! Ha! Ha!"

"Mister, I haven't got the time for all this now," Kamarin said, turning his attention back again to the bartender. "I need to know if any of you might have been fortunate enough to have met a man named Paladees. Malcome Poladees?"

"No, sir. I have never heard of him before."

"You know, somehow I could tell you hadn't," Kamarin said somewhat disappointingly and held up three fingers.

The bartender obliged and gave them their drinks.

Kamarin and his friends retreated to a corner and kept their backs to the wall.

Everyone in the crowded room still found a way to keep their own distance from the newcomers, not wanting to join the three who were asleep on the floor.

Except for one curious looking stranger who was bold in his approach. He was a rough looking man with a full face of hair and a muscular build. His scruffy appearance gave the first impression of that of a vagabond. He wore a long black coat that splayed open to conveniently display an assortment of weaponry stuffed into his wide belt. Kamarin felt that this was to impress them. But it did not.

As the man approached, Lort lowered his hammer, and leered at the stranger.

Kamarin held Lort back.

"I could not help but hear that you are looking for someone by the name of Poladees?" the stranger asked.

"Yes… but how would someone like you come to know him?" asked Kamarin.

"Do you want me to tell you what I know of him, boy? Or do you want to continue to be judgmental?"

Kamarin was somewhat impressed with his speech, considering it did not fit his exterior.

"Should I?" Kamarin turned to his friends as if to ask for their permission to speak with the man.

"Then I take it, you have no need to know, do you?" he said and turned to leave.

"Wait!" At this point, with little time to waist, Kamarin could not afford any more games. "Is it a price you seek?"

The man turned and invited himself to sit down.

"Yes, I believe you can say that."

"Well, I knew it," Erin said, waiving her hands in the air in disgust.

"I want a ship!" The stranger said leering at Erin. "A ship with enough food and fuel to carry me to the next star system. I want the hell out of here. This place made me numb over fifteen years ago. This pestilence has sickened me to no end and I can't take it anymore."

"Who are you?" asked Kamarin.

"Does it matter? I was no one twenty-two years ago, and then, for a little while, I was someone. When the man you seek became my friend. We fought together in the Great War and traveled together. We were quite a formidable pair." The stranger turned a little smile as he turned his drink and stared into it.

"What do you mean you traveled together?" Kamarin asked.

"Before the war with the Gorin slime dogs, we were captured and managed to escape. During that time we became good friends, you see, he had been injured and I had to take him to our village to hide. There we were again attacked and he died in my arms. He was a man with integrity, this one you seek. One who I will not soon forget."

"I'm not sure I understand. Was that Malcome Poladees?"

The man became a bit suspicious and suddenly decided not to offer much more information, voluntarily. "Well, maybe, and then again, I could be a little confused."

"You just said that you would never forget him," said Erin.

"Hmm! I did, didn't I?"

"Yes, you did," said Lort.

Both of them were beginning to show some irritation.

"There is talk that you could be the Guardian. How do I know that you are?" the stranger asked.

"It should be enough for you to just know!" Lort said, showing signs he was becoming annoyed with their conversation.

"I cannot say who I am, and if you are looking for proof, if I am trustworthy, I haven't any. But if it is important for you that I am, then I say I 'am." The stranger said taking a sip.

"You do not talk like a Guardian." Lort spoke gruffly.

"I am sorry if you don't approve, but I did not choose my destiny.

"If you have information for us, then I would appreciate it, but if you don't, then please- we have too much to do and not much time," Kamarin told the stranger, as he was getting up to leave.

"OK! You may be who you say you are. I only pray that you 'are'. Yes, I knew Paladees. He was once a Guardian of Thelona, a great and powerful man. We could have defeated them but everything changed so fast."

"What is your name?" Kamarin asked.

"Decker."

"Decker…what?"

166

"I have only kept my first name because I didn't like what 'some' wanted to call me."

"I understand."

"Since you are Guardian, there can be only one thing you would be looking for and I think I can help you, but it's going to cost you."

"A ship?"

"Yes."

"If it is what I need and you can prove to me to be an asset, then I will deliver it to you, 'personally.'" Kamarin raised his glass in agreement and gulped down its contents to wash the sand from his dry throat.

"One other condition," said Decker.

"And- what's that?" Kamarin asked cautiously.

"I get to help kill the Gorin."

"Of course! I wouldn't think of allowing anything less."

The two men 'clinked' their glasses together and smiled.

Kamarin's friends stood back a little, biting their lips. How could he invite a total stranger to join them in their quest? After all, he could be a spy. Even if it was evident they needed help, and if Decker was to join them, it should have been a decision made by 'all' of them. Hopefully, Kamarin could sense something in him that they could not.

"Ten"

Erin was not comfortable with Kamarin's decision to allow a perfect stranger to be such an important influence in their plans to stop the Gorin. Decker as he called himself, certainly couldn't be trusted.

It had been two days and still he had not arrived. Erin was busy in her thoughts as she jerkily made her way to the center of the under river city in her treader.

Even though the ride in her machine was rough, it seemed to have a calming effect on her nerves, but she felt when it came to Kamarin, he did not.

She started by having one daydream after another of Kamarin and her living together happily forever. Except she would constantly remind herself of her physical condition and that he could never be burdened by her. In fact, she wondered if she was not a burden to him even now, but she cared for him too much to keep entertaining such thoughts. She could only hope he did not see her the way she often pictured herself. Sometimes it was in a junk pile along with her dilapidated machine.

Her mind was full to capacity with worry as she whizzed past Kamarin coming in from an adjoining tunnel.

He knew for her to have passed him so quickly and not even see him, that she had to be preoccupied with something. Especially being able to ignore the loud squeaking noise that was now coming from the track and wheels of her treader machine.

Kamarin could not totally understand the funny feelings he would get lately in his stomach every time he saw her. He felt the need to be by her side and to protect her as he did his mother. But by no means would he ever tell her. She was not the kind to ever allow him to coddle her.

He was in tune to his friend's feelings, perhaps a bit more then they thought. Kamarin knew of their apprehension for having asked Decker to join their ranks, but because of his dreams, he had been prepared for their meeting on Bandagoon. This stranger would prove to be very helpful in the battle that would be taking place soon.

As he himself became occupied by his thoughts, he was not aware that he had passed Lort in the aisle where there were many activities taking place. There were rows of tables where thousands of weapons were being assembled.

Lort did not, of course, notice Kamarin either, as he was busy with the stepped up construction of many different new war machines that were now desperately needed.

He adopted the responsibility for the timely completion of each piece. His loyalty to his friends would always come first and foremost in his mind, his own family, his own race, were no more. He had adopted Erin, and he would be there now for the Guardian. Lort did not want revenge for his people, his- were not vengeful beings, and were generally peaceful, but he was determined to be instrumental in the demise of this Gorin race of beings. Because of their ruthlessness nature, Lort knew that the Gorin would not hesitate to annihilate other races to reach their sinful goals. Knowing this became his driving force. His main purpose for remaining close by was that of protecting Erin, wherever she might go. And after all, she was his people's only hope. If it were not for her, they would not have found the Guardian. Yes indeed, this was now his new home.

All three of them went about their busy schedules of helping prepare for the eminent attack of the Gorin.

They tried to wait patiently for Decker to come to the city but he still had not shown himself. After all, he and Kamarin had agreed that they would all meet here, then Decker would take them to search for Paladee's metal man.

It had been more than enough time for Decker to make it to the city. Erin started to persuade Kamarin into thinking that he would not show and that they should go and look for it themselves. Instead, Kamarin tried to reassure her that he would come and to be patient, but time was not on their side now, and Kamarin was starting to feel impatient himself.

He informed his guards to bring word as soon as he arrived.

Nightfall would soon be upon them once again, and still… no Decker.

Kamarin decided he would take a stroll along the top of one of the city's walls near its main gate. He hoped that he might be able to see if anyone was coming towards the city.

"Nice night for a walk sir, isn't it?" asked one of his men, when they met on the walkway at the top of the wall.

"Yes, it is," he said, with a minimum amount of attention, as he glared off into the horizon wondering where Decker might be. Could the Gorin have arrested him after their meeting on the sand moon? Kamarin knew that the men, who had secretly left the tavern that night, were somehow connected with their enemy. Did they cause Decker any harm?

While he gazed into the evening sky, he eventually realized that his centurion was in a quiet conversation with someone else, partially hidden in a shadow cast from a nearby building. It wasn't until he heard his name mentioned that he realized who it was.

"Decker! Is that you?" he asked.

The man dressed in all black came forward into the starlight and let himself be seen by Kamarin.

"Decker it is you! When did you arrive?"

"I arrived just this instant."

"Oh, of course you did my newly found friend. You undoubtedly have some power that I am not aware of yet- heh?"

"Not so, only my transport," Decker smiled and led Kamarin to the edge of the wall- motioning him to look over the side.

When Kamarin, smiling, glanced over the wall, he was startled by what he had just seen and jumped back.

There on the other side, sticking to the mossy covered stone was a giant lizard creature licking the air and staring directly into his eyes.

Kamarin stumbled, falling back to a sitting position on the walkway. "Wha-at-s-sat?" he asked Decker, pointing, with wide eyes.

"That, my friend, is the fastest and the most quietest form of transportation on this planet. Or for anywhere, I'd spect. They are called 'Slitheress Megalooness', because they hunt mostly at night. Great creatures, aren't they?"

"Uh-huh…huh?" Kamarin stared back at the wall.

"Fast lizard," Decker smiled.

"Oh." was all he could say, still not sure what Decker was saying, "you mean we're going to ride on that thing?"

"Yep! Oh, but you will have one of your own. I brought three more with me, they're down there," he said, pointing beyond the city's gate to a large group of trees.

"Why did you bring three?"

"Well, I'm sure your friends will want to join us, won't they?"

"One of them, yes. The other will find it too difficult to make the journey on one of those."

"She doesn't have any legs, does she?" Decker asked.

"Oh- um, no- she doesn't."

"That's why the machine, eh?" he said as he stroked his beard, deep in thought. "Well," he said as he put his hand on Kamarin's back and led him down some stairs, "we'll think of something."

Kamarin wasn't sure what he meant but he was glad that Decker had kept his promise.

"Say! What are you going to do about your..." Kamarin pointed back towards the wall where the creature was still clinging.

"Oh, he'll just return to the others and they'll go find food somewhere. They have great eye-sight at night you know, and they especially love Gorin!"

They continued their conversation chuckling as they disappeared down the moonlit stairway to the city's street below.

As was expected, Erin decided that she would have to stay behind this time due to the group's new mode of transportation. She really didn't like reptiles much anyway.

While Kamarin and his friends, waited for Decker to guide Kamarin and Lort on yet another expedition, they sipped their cool drinks by a fountain in one of the many garden pubs in the underground city; trying as they might to forget about the Gorin threat.

Their conversation was light and most of the subjects were only understood between Kamarin and Erin; evidently due to the physical attraction they shared. Kamarin would often smile and tried not to let his eyes say more than they should.

Erin felt comfortable with Kamarin going off and leaving her behind this time, but made it clear that he was not to leave her the next time. She was comfortable however, until Decker showed up.

He had brought with him a friend. She was tall with blond hair, beautiful features, blue eyes, and was scantily dressed.

As soon as Erin saw her, her guard was raised. Erin felt her face flush as she held back her defensiveness. But not for long as they soon approached their table.

"Who's your friend, Decker?" she asked, chewing on her lower lip.

"Oh, this is Ray," Decker replied.

"Ray? Is that a boy's name?" Erin asked, this time with a half chuckle.

"She is named Ray because she is like a ray of sunshine," he eloquently replied.

"I'll bet," Erin said, looking away in disgust and torment.

Kamarin was not sure what to make of the sudden situation with Erin. She had never before acted this way. He began to feel hot and his breathing was restricted.

"Is she your wife?" asked Kamarin.

"Hugh?" Erin huffed.

"No, she is my companion." Decker smiled petting ray's lovely hair.

"Hello," the woman said as she reached out to greet Erin.

"Hi! I'm Kamarin's companion," Erin said, pointing to Kamarin watching him out of the corner of her eye.

"Then you must be Kamarin, the great Guardian," she said, holding her hand out to greet him.

Erin looked at Kamarin and batted her eyes. "Time will tell, honey!"

"Well, don't you think we should be going?" asked Decker.

Erin's insides were beginning to burn hot. She never wanted to be with Kamarin more. Now that she might have to keep him out of trouble. Her emotions had betrayed her almost as much as her body.

As Erin watched the four of them ride out of sight, her tears welled up and ran down her cheek.

The old scientist Tresodin was there also to see them off, and could not help but observe Erin's reaction. He realized the only reason she stayed behind was because of her disability. He also knew that her machine would not last much longer and he did promise her he would help. Only, what to do? What to do?

Erin passed him partially hiding her face with her flowing brown hair. With her eyes to the ground, she made her way to the city's entrance.

"Erin!" Tresodin called to her but she did not, or chose not to hear as her machine squeaked inside the gate. His heart went out to her.

This time their destination would take them to the side of Thelona farthest from the sun. Normally, it would take many days to get there, but Decker was right, with these creatures it would not take half the time.

Their speed was incredible, the lizards were so fast, they were forced to wear scarves over their faces to be able to breathe. The seats they were strapped in actually were quite comfortable and made of thickly

175

padded leather. Metal rings had been pierced into the soft tissue- of what was evidently was the creatures' ears, along with the lead ropes the rider was able to steer. Rarely would the great lizard beasts stray from their paths, unless of course they became hungry; when that happened, a rest was required to allow them time to feed. It did become a hazard to try to stay on the zigzagging animal as it attempted to catch small birds and other small critters.

While they camped, Kamarin tried to be social and strike up a conversation with Ray- talking mostly about Erin and how the two of them met. But he was confused and did not understand why she would not look at him much.

Since it was dark they all made their beds for the night- except Ray. All of the answers for her strange behavior became apparent however, when Decker, before lying down to sleep, commanded her to keep watch for the night and her eyes suddenly became translucent.

"A robot!" said Kamarin.

"More than a robot-she was genetically engineered and she is my companion." Decker replied.

As Kamarin laid on the ground gazing into the night sky, he couldn't help but wonder how Erin would feel now if she knew that her feared competitor was but a machine?

The next morning before the sun had a chance to rise over a nearby mountain range, still very much in the dark, Decker suddenly was awaken with a large hand covering his face pinning him to the ground.

Lort was holding him and would not let go of him for fear he would yell out.

Decker flailed about making muffled noises but could not loosen Lort's grip.

Kamarin and Lort were waiting for a possible attack. Then when all was deemed safe, Kamarin looked to Decker.

"Lort! Lort! You'd better let him go, I don't think he's breathing!"

Lort looked down and with a surprised look he quickly released him.

"What the hell do you think you're doing?" Decker gasped.

"Shh!" Lort raised his large finger to his lips.

"What do you mean, shh? You nearly suffocated me!" Decker said trying to catch his breath.

"He said be quiet!" Kamarin said.

"Why?"

"Because your companion is no where to be found, that's why!" Kamarin answered as he searched in the darkness around the parameter of their camp.

"Oh- well, she can take care of herself, except it is a bit odd, her to leave and not report to me first, and in the middle of the night like this."

Kamarin looked at Lort and armed himself with a mini laser. "Can I read em' or what?" asked Kamarin.

"You've always had my vote, Guardian," Lort replied.

Kamarin leaned against a tree at the edge of camp and then produced a pair of night glasses from his pack and scanned the brush beyond.

"Well?" asked Decker.

"There 'is' something moving out there about a hundred meters away but I can't tell what it is,"

Kamarin said, motioning to Lort to go to a flanking position to investigate.

Once they located the source of the disturbance, it became evident they could be attacked at any moment. Ray- or what was left of her, lay before them in tangled mass of a shell- only tubing and wires from her waist down, her legs a few feet from her chest were twisting out of control.

"Who? What? Why would anyone do this to her?" asked Decker pulling a handful of wires from her mid section to make it stop. Then, he too became on guard selecting a weapon from his belt.

"I don't know who but I've got a feeling they really wanted one of us," said Kamarin.

"You think?" asked Decker.

While they waited for an ambush to come, nothing happened. Decker picked up the remains of his robot and headed back to camp, "I wouldn't stay out here long, the Gorin couldn't have done this, they're too afraid of the dark." he said.

Lort gave cover as he and Kamarin followed.

Decker was busy strapping what was left of his companion to the saddle of his lizard.

"What are you doing that for?" asked Kamarin.

"Because I'm not leaving her here. She can be repaired. She has been with me too long for me to just up and abandon her now."

Kamarin did not interfere and was thankful Erin had not come this time around. Even though they had not gone far, they still had learned a great deal. Their enemy was close, very close.

-*-

Tresodin searched through the underground city trying to locate Erin. He felt concerned about her being alone right now. When he finally did find her, she was in one of the central gardens. Its light was fed to it by reflected light from the surface.

Erin had separated herself from her machine and was lying in the soft green grass, listening to the rush of sea-water feeding through the huge conduit that was the river's huge fountain. The sound sent soothing waves over her as she basked in the mirrored sunlight. She struggled in her mind not to dwell on the fact that her friends were not close by, especially Kamarin. Unfortunately, her thoughts were indeed focused.

"Hello, Erin. I hope I am not interrupting?" Tresodin asked.

"No! Uhm, not at all," Erin said with a little faked yawn as she then tried pulling herself up into her machine trying to avoid his eyes. She quickly gave up and just leaned back on her hands.

"Please. You do not have to, on my account." he said.

"Don't be silly. I just needed the exercise," Erin insisted. "What's wrong? Is Kamarin all right?"

"Oh, it's not about Kamarin, Erin. To tell you the truth, I've been worried about you. How have you been my dear lady?"

"I haven't any problems to speak of, Tresodin. Why do you ask?"

"Kamarin will make you a good husband, and you a good wife," he said putting his hand on her shoulder.

"What makes you think that? I may not even be interested. Besides, Kamarin would do better by another," she said, shaking her head and turning away.

"That is where you are wrong, Erin Noble. That is where you are wrong."

"What do you mean?"

"Just promise me to be patient and hold that pretty chin up for the meantime, O.K.? I promised you that I would help and I will- soon."

"But how? Can you really do that?"

"I will, Erin, if it is the last thing I do."

"Oh, thank you, Tresodin. You are indeed a good friend." Erin smiled from ear to ear.

"Well, honey, please don't thank me yet, at least not until you properly benefit, all right?"

"OK!" she said as she quickly pulled herself up to her machine and for about the millionth time zipped herself in. With a smile she waved and sped off.

You had better deliver on this one, Tresodin thought as he made his way back to the others to help prepare for the impending attack.

-*-

The perimeter of the camp, the three of them were guarding, now was shrouded in darkness. It had been awhile since the destruction of Decker's robot companion. And now all of their heightened awareness had diminished to that of being pestered by the area's rather large insects. The threat was still there though, however they made it less of a priority now.

Kamarin built a fire to take the chill off and to provide them with a little light. Their shadows from it danced around the surrounding trees and transformed them into giants.

It was earlier than they thought, for the sun still had not yet risen.

As the incident became more of a historical event, they calmly sat by the fire they shared strips of smoked fish and meat. Kamarin loved eating meat, it was a food he; could not live without.

"Where are you taking us, Decker?" asked Kamarin.

"To a sacred place."

Kamarin looked to Lort as if he were asking him 'where'?

Lort just shrugged his massive shoulders.

"It is a place where my people, my tribe, have put to rest their loved ones, so that they can leave their bodies and go to the creator."

"Why there, Decker?" Kamarin asked.

"Because that is where I hid it."

"How far is this place?" asked Lort.

"It is not very- shh! Did you hear something?"

"What?" asked Lort. His eyes suddenly widened.

"Those high pitched sounds!

They seem to be coming closer!" added Kamarin.

"Correct, prepare yourselves! I know what it is!" Decker commanded.

"What is it?" asked Kamarin.

"Attack drones, they'll be coming from over there!" he said, pointing to the camp's opening through the trees.

"Hurry, put out the fire!" Kamarin motioned to Lort.

"Won't help!" Decker said as he gave both of them two more weapons he quickly chose from his belt.

As the targets appeared, one, then two, sped tumbling into camp. Decker yelled, "Shoot for your lives!"

The odd shaped drones tumbled over anything in their way as they came into camp. Lighting up the darkness with their streams of red laser blast coming from their crystal-like appendages. Each of them exploded into a more powerful display of lights when Kamarin and his companions hit their marks. The exhibit of fire could be seen for miles away as the battle erupted.

What seemed like hours were merely minutes until it was finished, the camp- suddenly became the attacking drone's graveyard. Each of them, once as big as a man, lay all around them. After the hype of it all, the three of them began to assess the situation.

"I have not seen one of these since the 'great' war!" said Decker.

"Well, I think now you will probably start to see them more often," Kamarin said as he counted the last one. "Eight, its a cinch someone knows we're here. This is not just a chance happening."

"I would say it's a safe bet," Decker agreed.

"What are you doing?" Lort asked as Kamarin laid down by the campfire covering himself with his mother's shawl.

"Getting some sleep," he said rolling over and almost immediately began to lightly snore.

"He is right," Decker said as he, too laid down to sleep.

But Lort was still trying to calm himself down after the excitement of the attack. Unable to sleep, he decided to keep watch for any other uninvited guests.

The next morning they all had put the evenings incident behind them. Except Lort was now host to two rather large, red eyes, and found it somewhat difficult to close them. Mounting their beasts, it was clear that he was a bit aloof.

It was quite hot this particular morning but they would be crossing several rivers today and the cool waters would be a welcome sight.

Almost as soon as they were saddled, they were off again.

The air became cooler when they did finally reach the marshy grasslands surrounding the large ponds, those of which the lizard beasts traveled over quite easily. Since they ran so fast when they hit the water, it was as if it wasn't even there. Kamarin likened it to skipping stones, something he could have been found doing when he was a child on L-2.

Before crossing the last body of water in their journey, they decided to rest on its banks. This was not one of the many ponds but a strange river connecting them. After they had cleaned themselves by its water, they were deciding to make camp when first they decided to go for a swim.

Lort made camp.

At the river's edge, Kamarin and Decker fell into conversation. Since Kamarin really knew very little about him, he felt a need to ease his curiosity.

"So tell me, Decker, what's your story?"

"You're a very trusting individual, Kamarin Mitchel, to have traveled this far with someone only to now be asking that question."

"Well, you see, I see it like this. Everyone or everything, I meet with, wants one of two things, either they want to kill me or they are content with just plain making my acquaintance. And in even that case- they may find a reason to want to kill me."

"Ha! Ha! Ha! For one so young, you are so right, but believe me, Kamarin, to be one of the latter. But I choose 'not' to kill you."

As the two of them enjoyed the soothing buoyancy the water provided, they decided to swim out from shore. They slowly drifted down stream and out of view of camp and Lort's protective eye.

"My tribe of people were a content race and took only what they needed from the land. Mind you, only what they needed. Your people were a kind and 'gentle' people and they allowed us to enjoy the simple pleasures in our lives.

"You see, our race guarded Thelona's natural beauty and all of its treasures. We listened to the land. When it yielded, we rejoiced in it. And when it wept, we wept. Thelona was home to many of our people. Just as you are Guardian of the galaxy, Kamarin, we were the same for Thelona. Even as much as we were content to do these things, some of us saw the need to do even more. That is why I helped the other Guardian."

Kamarin smiled to show his new friend his thankfulness, but suddenly took notice that they had moved down river.

"We should get back to camp," he said.

But when Kamarin turned back around to address Decker, he had disappeared, leaving only a ripple.

Then… "Kamarin!" Decker popped up from the now muddied water, swinging his arms wildly. But as quickly as he came up he went down again.

As Kamarin dove down to try to save him, he could not believe his eyes. A large river eel had Decker by the leg and was trying to pull him into his den into the side of the river's bank.

Kamarin swam immediately to the surface and yelled for Lort. Then he again dove to try to free him from the fish's jaws. But with lightening speed, the fish let go only for a second, long enough to snap at Kamarin and grab hold again of his drowning friend. Kamarin grabbed Decker to keep his head above water but the eel was too strong.

With little time to spare, Lort came to the rescue and leaped into the river with them. The sudden displacement of the surrounding water washed the giant fish from its hole. Lort and Kamarin were then able to drag Decker to shore. The two of them had their hands full as the giant fish twisted, trying to pull Decker down again. All of a sudden, one of the lizard beasts came from nowhere and clamped its huge jaws around the eel. The long fish arched in pain as the lizard gulped it down, licking its lips.

When they all caught their breath again…"See why I picked this form of transportation?" Decker asked with a grin.

"I personally wouldn't travel any other way." Kamarin said as he fell back in the mud.

Decker finally led them to another wondrous area of Thelona. A lush, green, grassy valley between two of the most beautiful mountain ranges they had ever seen. Snow covered their peaks at one even altitude enticing dreamers. The valley floor was unusually covered with many large stones of approximately the same size. Each of them probably weighed two hundred pounds or more, all of them lay in an even pattern. In the distance carved in the mountain's cliffs were numerous caves. It was evident that a once intelligent race had lived there.

"Is this where you lived?" Kamarin asked Decker.

"This is where I was raised," he said.

"Where are your people now?"

"The Guardian and I helped bury the last family under that stone over there," he said, pointing at one of the many thousands now partially covered by a thick mossy growth.

"You mean?" Kamarin struggled for words.

"Yes. Each stone represents a family who has died and is buried here," he said, climbing down from high upon the lizard beast's back. He then walked over to one of the stones, pointed at it, and looked to Lort to move it. Without much labor, Lort used one hand to unearth it and roll it to the side. Decker knelt down and removed what looked like a small bundle of rags from beneath it.

"Is that it?" asked Kamarin.

Decker walked over to him, bowed his head, and gave him the bundle. "This belonged to a great friend. Now it is yours. Please, use it as it was intended. Destroy the Gorin and set us free." Decker then climbed back onto his lizard and quickly disappeared down through the valley.

"Where is he going?" asked Lort.

"He is a strange fellow, isn't he?" Kamarin said as he un-wrapped the metal man from his cocoon of rags. "But he is full of heart."

Upon their return, Kamarin stood on a plateau that overlooked the Thelonan river-city.

No life signs were noticeable, and that was exactly what he expected. It was a good sign his people had remained undetected.

It was twilight now and it would remain this way for the rest of the night, because of the amount of stars in the sky.

Kamarin felt he was now ready to face Voltar, even though he still had not located the last of the metal men. Four of the metal giants would surely be enough force to defeat his army, he thought.

Kamarin held the new metal man to the sky. "Mother! I now have two more of the metal men. Once again the creator smiles upon us. Father! Take heart to know that it is your light that guides me now and I thank you for it. Please, Father! Mother! Be with me now!"

"Eleven"

Having completed most of the heavy priority work, Kamarin's people were enjoying their return home more and more. Except for some finishing touches, the people of Thelona were prepared for the attack of the Gorin.

As Kamarin passed a group of young men standing in line for their turn to try out their newly acquired forms of self-defense, he noticed that Lort had volunteered to be the opposition, or punching bag, in laymen's terms. Kamarin turned to walk away when he heard the familiar thud of Lort's body hitting the ground, followed by a long groan. Lort easily could have overpowered any or for that matter, all of the young cadets, but someone had to take the place of missing training equipment.

It had been over two months since Kamarin had seen Erin but there was a simple explanation. Everyone had a project to complete before the defense of their home planet would be effectively protected from their enemy. But Kamarin could not remember what task Erin had taken. And why hadn't she been staying in contact with him? Now he was starting to worry.

The centurion at the entrance to the city had also reported that Decker had returned, and was somewhere inside. Why was he, too being so elusive? What could be so important that they seemed to be intentionally eluding him, with all of these questions weighing heavy on his mind, he decided to search for the old scientist, Tresodin. Even 'he' was becoming hard to locate. Fortunately Tresodin had reported to the city's main computer as to his whereabouts. Kamarin had discovered that Tresodin and even Decker had gone to the ancient part of the city and had been there for quite some time, but why?

The old part of their city was the place his ancestors had first begun building. Believing it to be unsafe it still had not been destroyed because it was rich in historical value. Even the power to that section had been turned off long before the 'great' war but Tresodin had for some reason restored a small quadrant.

Kamarin climbed down from one of the small lookout towers at the top of another of the city's walls overlooking the ancient section of the city. He was upset to see that the lights in this area could be seen through the river's deep water, especially by anyone orbiting Thelona. What did they think they were doing? Kamarin was beginning to think his friends had taken leave of their senses. It would serve them right if he shut down that section and left them in the dark.

But instead he would give them the benefit of the doubt and decided to investigate further. At least he should let his friends explain why they had put the whole city at risk of detection.

Angrily he made his way deep into the underground portion of the old city and searched room to room.

His ancestors had built this end of the city thousands of years ago. It was surprising to him that any of the amenities still operated. They truly were an advanced race to have created many of them to last this long.

As he stepped quickly from a moving walkway he noticed some intriguing art-work of their era. They were indeed great craftsmen. Without question there were many skills that had been long forgotten. The architects must have been interesting people. Their forgotten skills could be an immense value today.

But as Kamarin journeyed farther, it was evident that time had not been kind to its structures and the area was really not safe. The hallway's walls were covered with algae, pillars and other surrounding walls were covered with sweat because of the river being so close above.

Kamarin suddenly heard voices coming from the end of the long corridor. He recognized Tresodin's immediately and he was talking to another who could be Erin.

When he walked into the room, he noticed a beautiful shaped woman with her back turned towards him in conversation with the old scientist.

"Excuse me, Tresodin, but have you seen Erin? I haven't talked with her in awhile and I'm beginning to get concerned," Kamarin finished, just then the woman turned to face him.

"Hello, Kamarin. So, you've been worried about me, huh? Why, I've been here all along."

"Kamarin was stunned. Erin stood before him almost eye to eye. She was host to one of the biggest smiles he had ever seen on her pretty face.

"Erin, but how? I don't understand?" Kamarin sat back in disbelief.

"Tresodin did it for me! Do you like them?" she asked. Turning around to allow him to inspect her new legs.

"But- how did…?"

"Well, I guess we have Decker to thank, really. After all, they did once belong to his robot. Instead of having her rebuilt, he donated them for what I might say, is a most worthy cause," Tresodin said with a smile of his own.

"Well, do you like them, Kamarin?" Erin asked a little more seriously this time.

"Their beautiful, Erin, but it is who they are now attached to that makes them that way," said Kamarin.

"Oh, Kamarin." Erin threw herself at him, hugging him hard. "I am so happy," she said crying.

"Her legs are those of an android now but with the use of the ancients' technology, I was able to implant a genetic seed that will reconstruct their molecular structure and make them more hers with each day." The old scientist could see that neither of them really, were listening to him and he felt he was no longer needed. Quietly, Tresodin left them alone.

"I love you, Kamarin."

"I haven't loved anyone more, Erin," he said.

-*-

Only an elite few gathered in the grandiose reception center created for the leaders of the Gorin to be entertained while they sat boasting of their conquests. Ogel was always in his height of glory and in full conceit. But today he and Voltar would sit alone at one of the outer tables he had carefully selected, far away from the senate staff and their new leader.

Voltar was slightly disturbed by the change in seating arrangements, since it was always Ogel's wish to sit as close to the ruling class as he could. It was not like Ogel at all. Suspicious, though curious to see what he might have planned, Voltar, surrounded by a few of his soldiers, took his place reserved by Ogel at the table.

"Why do you sit so far away, Ogel? You know they cannot see you very well from over here. You should have picked a table much closer," said Voltar, pointing.

"I don't think you would want to sit where they're sitting tonight," replied Ogel.

"Why? What do you mean?"

"I mean that after tonight, you will once again take your place as leader of the Gorin."

"The people follow me now!"

"Oh, how wrong you are Voltar, their military takes your orders all right but they do not look up to you anymore. You're old and twisted. They have a new puppet. One that squeaks when expected. Oh, far be-it for these people, having any allegiance to you now. But they will again after tonight, I'm willing to wager."

"Just what is it you plan to do then?"

"Just watch and be ready to announce to the people that 'you' are in control."

As the senate entered the large ballroom, making their way to a long table prepared especially for them, the Gorin people stood applauding.

After the senators took their places, the rest were then permitted to sit down.

Ogel picked up his glass and raised it to Voltar. "Don't be so nervous. It will be any time- now!" he said with a smile.

Just then the ground started to shake under the senators' table. Everyone except Ogel panicked. Ogel tried to pay the incident no attention and took another sip of his drink with some dribbling down his chin.

Voltar could tell by Ogel's reaction that this was the beginning of his plan. Shaken, Voltar's eyes were wide while both hands clamped to their table when the ground beneath them rumbled. As afraid as he was, he eagerly waited for what was yet to come.

A large glittering cloud enveloped the leaders of Gore as the crowd scattered. With every horrified eye upon them, the cloud started to shrink, imprisoning them. They seemed to be suffocating by it. Smaller and smaller the cloud closed in on them, until it disappeared. Now in more of a panic the crowd became fearful, that they would be next.

Ogel then stood up and started clearing a path for Voltar to follow him to the very place where the senators had just vanished.

Voltar then stood in front of them, demanding everyone's attention.

"Stop, stop this foolishness! Stop this immediately!" he said waving his arms wildly.

When they realized that the ground had not returned shaking for them, they finally began to calm down and listen to Voltar.

"Now, that is better. Some unknown force has taken our leaders from us. Until we find out where they might have gone, I am assuming full control. You will once again put your faith in me. There is absolutely no need to worry for I, Voltar, will protect you. Now go from this place for we have much to do to prepare ourselves for our last great battle for Orion! Yes, now go! Go and prepare to attack!" Voltar finished his triumphant speech waving at them to leave the reception hall.

Ogel was amused at the way Voltar handled himself with the Gorin, crude but effective to say the least.

"Hey, boss, that was great!" Ogel said patting him on the back. "But I don't think they're coming back. No, in fact, I know they're not," Ogel said, chuckling as he finished the last of his drink.

"What do you mean? What did you do with them?"

"Didn't you see what happened to them? I used a 'deft bomb! An imploding particle bomb. For them it was quite humane, whatever that is. They never felt a thing. At least I don't think they did."

"But how did you get it in here without being seen to plant it?"

"I have ways. Believe me, I have my ways." Ogel dropped his glass at Voltar's feet and disinterestedly walked away.

Voltar then came to the realization that he had again regained his right of leadership, however now he would have to watch his own back very carefully. Ogel reminded him too much of himself, and he had become almost as powerful, but his own experience would help him defeat even this young threat in the end.

Actually the people of Gore were happy that Voltar was again in control, because they loved war as much as he did.

He inspected the command center again as he did so often before, pacing back and forth between the two long aisles of computer stations. Everything, of course, was going as planned, like he had never left. Yet, he felt uneasy for some reason. Suddenly he heard something.

"What is that sound?" He zeroed in on it the way any good predator would. Stopping at one of the communication terminals, he grabbed the radioman by his shoulder.

"Sir, can I help you?" the radioman said shaken.

Voltar just moved in closer and turned an ear to listen to the sound box.

"Where is that coming from?" Voltar barked.

"What, sir?" the soldier started to shake nervously.

"That!" he said pointing. "Never mind. Get up and let me have it."

The Gorin soldier jumped to attention as Voltar sat feverishly moving dials. "There- I know what it is! Yes, of course I do and indeed, and 'you' would not. Not, with your limited brain capacity. Oh yes, there it is…a sweet sound at that. Yet, I'm not quite sure how it was done but never the less it has been activated! It's unmistakable! They're calling us home!" Satisfaction filled Voltar's eyes. "It is too bad they will not like 'my' returning home. It has been long enough, now I will finish it before we proceed to the outer planets." He could not have been more thrilled, swinging his arms like a child as he started to walk away.

"What's up?" asked Ogel, arriving at the terminal.

"I'm going home that's what!" Voltar grinned.

"Hum?" was Ogel's only reaction.

"That's right. Your friend calls to me and soon I will answer," Voltar said, using the back of his hand to move Ogel aside. Then proudly he walked out of the command center.

Ogel thought a minute. "Kamarin!" he said as he too left, angrily.

-* -

The Guardian knew better than to leave the protection of the city, but he and Erin decided to leave its confines just for a short ride into the grassy hills beyond its gates.

It was early morning and from their vantage-point the sun could be seen lighting up the valley from one end to the other.

The two of them had dismounted from the lizards to lie in the lush, green grass that waved gently in the warm breeze.

"Kamarin."

"Yes, Erin?"

"Do you think that I've been acting childish?"

"I'm not sure, it has been a long time since I have been a child to be able to compare you to one."

"Oh, Kamarin, you know what I mean. I've been acting selfish and sometimes stubborn."

"Sometimes?" Kamarin said, turning his head and smiling.

"Kamarin, I'm serious," she said, elbowing him in the ribs.

"Ooof! Well, I thought you wanted me to agree." Grimacing, he quickly rubbed his side.

"No. As a matter of fact, you were supposed to disagree."

"I'm sorry. Next time tell me what I am supposed to do, OK?"

"Oh well, you know what I mean. I mean the way I acted when I met Ray. I was jealous of her. I was jealous of her beauty. Of her being more beautiful than me and having legs. These legs!" she said lying back on her elbows clicking her toes together.

"Erin. She was not more beautiful than you are, and those legs fit you better anyway. So, what are you trying to say?"

"I'm sorry, Kamarin, I am just having some regrets that's all. I just have not been much support to you, as much as I should have."

"Nonsense, Erin. If it were not for you, I wouldn't have come this far."

"I appreciate and love you for that, Kamarin, but I guess I'm trying to say that if we are to go on together from here, I want to do more for you," Erin said shyly.

"Just be with me, by my side, Erin. That is all I wish from you."

"From now on, Kamarin, I will not leave your side," she said, leaning over him kissing him gently.

But their embrace was broken by the sudden sound of the Thelonan fighters racing each other after taking off from one of the underground air-strips. Hundreds of them seemed to pour out of the single opening in the ground near the city like a swarm.

It was a spectacular sight that would not easily be forgotten, but then again who would want to?

The fighters filled the air in a mock battle, the noise, from their burning engines were almost deafening.

Kamarin and Erin just stood holding each other as they watched the most advanced fighting force in all of the Orion star system. Slowly the many dogfights ended and one after another, of the fighters returned to their home base.

"Do you think they knew we were out here?" Erin asked.

"After the exhibition they just gave us, I think it's safe to say- they did." Kamarin kissed her and helped her back into the saddle.

"Kamarin, I love our home."

"It is most wondrous isn't it?" he said and turned his beast toward the city. Erin's mount followed on its own. She had finally grown accustomed to the ride.

As they entered the city's gate, Kamarin had a familiar intuition come over him.

Looking down to his wrist that was growing warm, the metal man was starting to grow again- but faintly. Kamarin jumped from his lizard and quickly helped Erin.

When she too saw the metal man, she said nervously, "They're here!"

"No, not- yet! No matter how much I don't want them to come- they are on their way," Kamarin said, taking her by the hand leading her to an underground entrance.

Kamarin was almost out of breath by the time they reached the core of the city. On the other hand, Erin's new appendages performed flawlessly. Her increased breathing rate was due only to her excitement.

Kamarin coughed several times to catch his breath. Erin just smiled at him.

Lort met them at the same time Tresodin did. "Is it time?" Lort asked.

"Yes! But we will need to send out scouts to report any early arrivals," said Kamarin.

"We will have several of them work in shifts," Tresodin replied, saluting as he quickly left.

"Good! Lort, try to find Decker, I'll need both of you to lead key regiments from vantage-points that you, yourselves will have to determine.

"No one has seen him, Guardian, but I will find him," Lort said as he lifted his large new axe over his shoulder and went searching immediately.

It has been a long time since Kamarin saw Decker and he was not sure he was still in the city. He hoped he had not left Thelona. Because his experience with fighting the Gorin, Kamarin would sorely feel the loss if he were not there to help lead his people into battle.

Kamarin remembered where it was that he last saw him and yelled to Lort to change his direction. "Lort, the old city!" he waved to him.

"Erin! I'm putting you in charge of the safety of the women and children."

"Mmmm," she said. "OK. I guess I can handle that and still be by your side in battle," Erin replied.

"Uhm, no, you can…" Kamarin began to say but then realized the look he was receiving. "OK, but you must do what I tell you, all right?"

"Sure, I always do," she said with a smile.

"Tresodin! How many ground fighters do we have now?" Kamarin asked as if prepared to be disappointed.

"At least ten thousand. And more coming in every day! Most of them are like you. Children of the 'lost', returned." The old scientist crossed his arms, rocking, back and forth heel to toe as he smiled.

Kamarin was well pleased to hear that, but he also knew that preparedness was mostly a state of mind. Even though it seemed his army could well defend itself, and might even prevail, his mind was still not at ease.

"It's not going to be that easy," he said as he turned, leaving Tresodin and Erin alone.

"Something is wrong, "Tresodin said, shaking his head after Kamarin had left. Erin excused herself and ran quickly to catch up with him.

-*-

Behind this door is tons of water, pressing on it, trying to find a way through, Decker thought, as he inspected one of the living quarters of an ancient Thelonan.

This part of the city was once in great danger of being flooded and the bulkheads were constructed in case the water did find a path of least resistance. Now it seemed it could be.

Peering through the porthole in the bulkhead door, he could see algae and tall water grasses growing thick in the rest of the room beyond.

The whole bulkhead was sweating on the side of the room he was in. It has not been long since this process had been taking place, for there was no algae growth on his side of the window or bulkhead.

The bolts holding the massive wall together must be failing, he thought as he continued to check them. Some of the heads had been 'cut' half way through.

"A saboteur!" Decker said out loud after making the discovery. He knew that he very well might have interrupted the assassin by stumbling into the area, but maybe the cuts were made long before he had come to this city. Another quick inspection proved that that was not the case. The metal showed no signs of aging where the cutter left its marks. Only one answer was left.

"We have a traitor among us!" he said, again thinking out loud as he left the crewman's quarters with weapons drawn.

It had been sort of an open invitation to anyone who wanted to join forces with the Thelonans to spy on their trusting nature. Any agent could have easily infiltrated their ranks. This person who sawed through the bulkhead bolts had put the whole city in peril.

"Decker here! Send me six security police to the ancient personnel sector right away! Tell them to meet me…at the 333rd cubicle and do it on the double!"

I will not leave so that whoever you are might be free to finish what you have so eloquently started, he thought.

Decker ran through the lists in his memory of people he had met and who could be a suspect, unfortunately, none came to mind.

After he had waited a few minutes for the guards to arrive, he finally heard them far off, down the long dimly lit corridor.

"What was that?" he said as a noise came from behind. Slowly he went to investigate. Whoever it is, he is running towards me, he thought.

Thinking quickly, Decker hid himself in the shadows. Just as the heavy sounds of footsteps came closer they suddenly became familiar.

"Hey!" Decker yelled, causing the large shadow to jump back against the wall.

"What the," Lort said.

"Hey, what's up?" asked Decker.

"Where have you been? The Guardian has sent me for you. Well, come with me" Lort said waving his big hand. "We have things to do."

Decker met the security police and told them to wait for him there, and pointed to positions where he wanted them to take cover and watch for any intruder. Little did they know that all this time they were being watched from yet another shadow in the dark corridor.

Kamarin was initially pleased to see that Decker had not yet left, but he was definitely disappointed to hear about the traitor. More importantly, how many were there? And were they successful? That was his worry.

He decided that this new development was much too important to ignore and told Decker to find the traitor and bring him back to see him.

Decker promised he would not return to Kamarin without the traitor.

Yet there was still a larger, more threatening situation and Kamarin's concerns were confirmed by his engineers. The area above the ancient part of the city could not take many above ground explosions without collapsing and causing flooding to the rest of it.

Troubled with this new knowledge, he could not trust the underground to provide the safe haven for his people much longer. They were all going to have to be moved to a safer place before the battle began, perhaps to the dark forest in the Thelonan continent's interior?

That night, along with many of Kamarin's worries, he had a dream.

"It's cold! And very dark! What is out there? Who is out there?" Kamarin is yelling into the dark night. "I know there's someone there, show yourself to me now!"

There was nothing but the smell of death looming.

As if appearing from nowhere, a dark figure intent on running him through with a long-knife spear, charged straight for him, closing fast. Kamarin had little time to move. Just when he expected to feel the gut-piercing point of the blade, the sinister figure was suddenly struck down from behind.

Within seconds the darkness around Kamarin became brilliantly 'lit' and he became blinded by it.

Two large human figures stepped out of the light and stood before him.

When he regained some of his sight, he saw a very tall man and woman of at least eight feet. Both of them carried huge swords. The man leaned on his with the large tip dug into the ground. Evidently the woman had been the one who had vanquished the attacking figure and stood ready to use her sword again. But none other dared try again.

When Kamarin's eyes became clearer, he was shocked when he finally recognized them, but they were now twice as big as ever.

"Mother! Father! Where did you—? How did you—? How have you changed into this form?"

"Hello, my beloved son," his father said in acknowledgment.

"Kamarin! We have a battle to fight of our own. This life is parallel in the creator's service to yours. This war has been fought since the beginning of time. There have been many battles and we have won them all, till now. The power of the creator is very strong and we will win again. With his power, he uses us to triumph over evil. Much the same as he is using you," his mother said, as she too stabbed the ground with her mammoth sword, "he uses us".

"But I don't understand, mother. Are you not dead?"

"Yes, to you, but we have gone on to this life and here we continue to help our brothers in this world and the old."

"But why do you come to me?"

"So that you can be assured that you are not alone and you are being protected. Some day, Kamarin, you, too will stand with us in this life."

"But for this one, my son, you must live to the fullest," his father added.

Kamarin looked around quickly realizing he was in the other place where he once had disappeared before. It was the same white room with the one lone table. Except now a sword almost as long, lay down its center.

He could not stay away from the cool, blue haze of light that emanated from it. It drew him like the planet drew Bandagoon from the deep of space.

When he turned to his parents again, they were gone.

"Take it, Kamarin." It was his mothers voice again, sounding as if she were far away in a desert canyon. "Go on and take it, my son. It has been crafted especially for you by the angels of heaven. It was to be given to you when you join us in battle in this place but things have changed here. It is more important for you to use it in your world now to help us in ours. The creator will shield you. And the sword is his hand- the hand of GOD!" Her voice echoed as it escaped with the light, only to be replaced by another's.

"Kamarin! Kamarin! Wake up, Kamarin!" Erin shook him. He was drenched in his own sweat when he finally woke.

"You were having a terrible nightmare, Kamarin! I was afraid for you."

Kamarin stood up from his bed and walked across his room staring ahead.

"I don't think that it was a dream," he said as he gazed upon a large sword propped up in the corner with the ever-warming blue haze light surrounding it.

"Oh my! Kamarin, where did that come from? It wasn't here awhile ago."

"From the angels, Erin, from the angels."

"Twelve"

The metal men stood slightly larger than Lort as they stood guard in the control room while Kamarin and his friends discussed plans to defend Thelona from the Gorin scouts who were observed gathering in preparation of Voltar's arrival.

Fifteen days had gone since the first warning of an attack, given by Kamarin's metal man Deke.

The saboteur among his people had not been found and Decker was still hot on his trail. By voice transmission, he had delivered a message to Kamarin that they had decoded a homing device but were unable to locate its operator. Somewhere inside the city they knew they would find him hiding.

Several young men were sent to Kamarin, under arrest for secretly meeting at night in a park, but they were soon released having been absolved of any wrong doings. Kamarin was a little disturbed by them though, remembering how Ogel was easily swayed by Voltar's evil ways. Voltar had met him secretly in much the same way, and eventually taught him all too well how to be lower then the things that crawl.

Hovering in the control room was a holographic image of Thelona, the Gorin preliminary strike force had been seen just a day from their position. Several landing sights had been noted. Each of them would have to be neutralized before the Gorin could set up an outpost. They could not be allowed to prepare the way for their main assault force.

There would have to be night raids on these Gorin positions to take them by surprise, and avoid detection from any of their early arrivals.

It was decided that Kamarin and Lort would lead the attacks, but Kamarin faced one problem, they were both unfamiliar with Thelona's terrain. Trying to predict where the Gorin would infiltrate their defenses and ultimately amass an all out attack was difficult. After all, his home planet was very large and almost anything could take place on it without detection.

One thing was a probability though the fact that the Gorin would use their new version of the metal men was a good bet. If the information he had been receiving was true about the number the enemy possessed then his metal men stood a good chance of easily defending themselves. His metal men would, of course, be outnumbered, but the enemies' projected giant images were only as good as the Gorin behind them. In comparison, Kamarin's metal men had their own intelligence, of "sorts". It was indeed a great comfort to him that they could function on their own.

They did not require his direction for every move, could they think for themselves, possibly?

Kamarin's main concern though was for his people. He needed to do everything in his power to minimize their loss. His heart ached to know that some would be giving up their lives for the freedom of the rest. He, too, felt that this must be the last time the Gorin could be allowed to wage war again. To stop them from this, he knew that the numbers of their race needed to be greatly reduced.

The thought of it all was overwhelming and as Kamarin sat alone, he shed a tear for the inevitable loss both sides were going to suffer.

That night Kamarin, Erin, and Lort along with twelve Thelonan warriors made their way to the location where the Gorin scouts had been assembling.

As Kamarin's small group closed in on the sight where they had moored their fighting aircraft, he noticed Erin was on her knees quickly saying a prayer. For this was the night the battle for Orion would begin.

If the Guardian, and his people, would have been any later in their efforts to surprise the Gorin scouts, the Gorin would have had time enough to assemble most of their battle equipment.

The Gorin had a vast array of land fighting machines that would quite easily conquer any fighting force in the galaxy. That is except for the new Thelonan's. Though this group was heavily armed they still, were no match for the Thelonan fighters who were now occupying the city. All of this will be to the Gorin's surprise.

As Lort began the onslaught, wading through the enemy soldiers with his axe, Kamarin's metal men

209

grew slightly larger and started tearing up the parked fighter airships. The invaders tried to power up several of their hover-craft mounted artillery, but Kamarin quickly disabled them with just as many Landwheels, then- it suddenly turned to every man or woman to defend themselves.

Kamarin ran to Erin's side as they fought and killed all Gorin that came their way. Erin, armed with only a laser pistol and a long knife, was able to defend herself very well. Kamarin's sword was strapped to his back and he made no move to use it. He was too busy using his two Tonbouys and his pack of surprises. Within seconds, every Thelonan warrior was engaged in hand to hand fighting at the Gorin preemptive landing sight.

Because the element of surprise was on their side, they were able to defeat them without taking a loss of their own. When the fighting subsided, everyone was still in an elevated state of readiness. They had been prepared for more of a resistance but there obviously would not be any. The fighters raised up and began to cheer.

"Stop!" Kamarin yelled to them. He waved his knives at them. "Stop! Stop! We have just taken lives! Even though they are not human, they were still created by our god and we must not rejoice in having taken their lives. Do not gloat over them, for it is not over. It has only begun. It has only just begun..."

Having humbled the crowd of fighters with his sobering message, Kamarin turned to leave but stopped to address Lort.

"Lort, would you wait here until our burial team arrives?"

"Yes, Guardian, I will." Lort noticed Kamarin's voice had changed.

Kamarin separated himself from the others and sat upon a rock to watch the sunrise. He tried to block from his mind the terrible fight that was to come. Why was this all necessary, if his father was still alive he would have been living his life as an adult on L-2. As far as he knew, this battle would be the first his people had seen on Thelona. He could not let it be destroyed.

As Kamarin sat watching 'the sun light up his world, Erin and Lort joined him at his side. In silence, they took in all of its beauty that it was so gallantly offering them.

Then Kamarin slowly stood, still under its spell. "Well, it is time. I hope I will finally live up to your expectations. Those of which you had for me when you first found me," he said as he looked glassy-eyed at his friends.

"You are the Guardian, Kamarin Mitchel! You can be no less," Lort said, laying his giant hand on Kamarin's shoulder.

"Lort is right, Kamarin. With your mother's passing, the torch your parents were given to bear; is now yours. There is no living being that will be able to take it from you. You are 'truly' the Guardian, and I could not be more proud to be your friend," Erin said, and then kissed him on the cheek.

"P-l-lease! I am not some sort of god!" he said boldly as if her kiss had brought him back to life.

"No, you are not. But you do have a job to do," said Erin.

"Then I should do it."

Kamarin decided, since he was not familiar with his own home planet, he should go out on his own and physically reconnoiter it. So having requisitioned a fighter, he left his friends at the coastal city and headed inland to see the rest of Thelona for the first time.

Inside the cockpit of the fighter, only a light 'whir' could be heard from its engine.

As Kamarin looked around at the rolling hills disappearing into the horizon, the beautiful colors were dulled by the imitation image projected into his helmet's face shield. Although technologically crucial to aid in engaging the enemy in battle, the shield spoiled the view for any serious sightseeing, so he took it off.

To familiarize himself with the fighter's capability, he put it to the test as he rolled it flying low above the trees and other terrain.

Suddenly, he realized he had passed over one of the largest cities he had ever seen.

He quickly looped the fighter to return.

Slowing to a hover above it, Kamarin could not believe what he was seeing. There he was, over some of the tallest buildings in all of Orion. Rolling the craft slightly, he could see between them but could only barely make out the streets below. Not far from one of the huge buildings he tapped his altitude meter. He was astounded. The building was over a thousand feet high. And looking to the horizon the buildings stretched, disappearing into it.

"This city cannot be 'all empty," Kamarin said out loud. Then he began to wonder just how many more of these metropolises were here on Thelona. The story of the exodus his mother had told him about was not massive enough to have included all of the people here. Where could they have all gone?

Kamarin turned his ship around and started back towards the sea and the relatively small city his friends were taking refuge in.

Tresodin, better have some excuse for not telling me about this. If there are no people in that city, then where were they? Are they all dead? Kamarin searched for answers as he piloted the fighter home.

-*-

Dark, damp and laden with mosses of all different species, was the way the ancient city had been left since there had been no one for over twenty years to perform the necessary maintenance.

Because the lighting was very poor, Decker and his men used glasses that detected heat given off by living beings. The only problem they faced with them was that they could not tell friend from foe.

Decker had stationed two of his men deep in the abandoned area of the city. The two sentries made themselves literally a part of the green growth that was part of the walls, the ceiling, and the floor. The farther they traveled into it became so dense they could not walk easily. And the more prehistoric it became. If the soldiers were not dug in and camouflaged by the strange plant life, they stayed always in the shadows when they traveled.

Decker had assured them that if they were patient, they would be successful in capturing the saboteur, and he was right.

They were about to close in on him at any moment.

They had heard strange noises coming from the darkest part of the hallway covered heaviest with the weird growth. There was no doubt in their minds that the sounds must be coming from the assassin.

Beginning their assault, they radioed to report their situation to Decker who was busy with the rest of his men as they searched above ground.

"Captain Decker sir, sir! Come in, sir!"

"He probably didn't hear you- try it again!"

"Captain Dec."

"Yes, What is it, son?" Decker replied, temporarily holding up his own search- now in full progress.

"Sir, this is agent Crane. I think we've located our man, sir! He is farther into the old city than we thought. It sure sounds like he's up to something. Captain, should we go in?"

"What's stopping you? I thought you boys were calling me to tell me that you had already apprehended him."

"No, sir. I'm afraid not yet, sir. But next time we call you, that'll be our report!"

"Proceed!" said Decker.

The two elite and highly trained soldiers readied themselves with their laser rifles.

Slowly as not to draw attention to themselves, they moved into the darkness.

Then suddenly a strange sound came from what was suppose to be their destination.

The two soldiers quickly searched for their small but powerful emergency lights as a low growl came from directly in front of them. Having found the switches simultaneously, the flood of light brightly illuminated the object in their path, along with something else.

A giant 'algae worm'. At least it resembled one. But this one had TEETH, big razor-like teeth.

"Time to go!" said one soldier.

"Right behind you!" said the other as they slipped and slid on the slimy vines on their way out.

Luckily for the two soldiers, this beast was more interested in resting in the cool, dark and damp foliage. Running for daylight, they were so concerned with their self-preservation that they ran past the very person they were there to arrest. The saboteur had partially hidden himself as the men approached. Today was just his lucky day.

However, considering what had taken place he, too decided that it might not be very safe if he stayed. So, with yet another aggravated growl from the dark hallway, he made his hasty retreat.

Later that evening, Decker was getting close to solving the crime. There was no doubt that his investigation was about to pay off. His men had discovered that a man, by the name of Kotch, had been living alone in one of the apartments near the city's main gate. Clearly to allow him an easy escape. Surtronic transmissions in the Kiga band had led them to his place of residence. They definitely had their man and now it was time to see if he was home.

As some of Decker's men began to surround the building, a lonely light in the corner window was snuffed out.

Everyone froze waiting to see what his next move would be.

Since he just appeared to be hiding, Decker waved his men to advance. Having covered the front entrance, the traitor surprised them by throwing open the door, stepping out with his hands in the air submitting to them.

"It is over for you, traitor!" Decker said as they met face to face.

"For you and I, it does not matter. This planet will be dust," the criminal insisted.

"And you and I with it, friend," Decker said as he took the spy firmly by the back of the neck to escort him to a place of detention. "The Guardian will be very pleased to know we have you in custody."

"Ha! There are no more Guardians."

"You are not a very good spy then are you?"

A frightened look came over the prisoner's face.

"A Guardian? Here?"

"Yes, here. How lucky can you get, spy?" Decker said as they disappeared down one of the underground tunnels.

-*-

"Ms. Noble. We have the Guardian's location. He appears to be returning," one of the soldiers said as he monitored a console in the control room.

"Why would he be coming back so soon, Tresodin?" Erin asked, concerned that he might have already met up with Gorin foul play.

"I suspected that he might. Let's go and see what the problem is. How 'bout it?" he said.

The underground sky port was host to many different kinds of spacecraft. The majority of which were new Thelonan fighters that had been quickly manufactured. Because of limited space, each large fighter was stacked on a very large conveyor system. The system would efficiently launch each fighter with great speed in, an emergency. More than two hundred fighters could be in the air within minutes.

As the inner barrier doors opened, the ramp that would receive Kamarin's fighter was raised just moments before he landed. The ramp lowered, the blast doors closed. Then the attending receiving personnel returned to their normal duties.

Kamarin slowly stopped his aircraft in front of Erin and Tresodin, waiting patiently in the receiving area.

"Hello, Guardian. That was a short trip, is everything all right?" the Tresodin asked.

Kamarin threw his helmet to one of the flight assistants. "Come with me!" he ordered. "I have a few questions I would like answered."

Erin was confused but eagerly trailed behind, following them to one of the ready rooms. Kamarin seemed very angry. This was an emotional side of him she had only seen once before, the time when they had been captured by the Gorin and Kamarin came face to face with Voltar. She knew him to mean business then, and was sure he did now.

"All right, spill it!" said Kamarin, slamming the door behind them.

"What do you mean?" Tresodin replied.

"I want to know what has happened to all of our people? Those cities out there are big enough to house hundreds of thousands of people! Where have they gone, Tresodin?"

"I told a lie to you before, Guardian."

"Yes?"

"Voltar found many of our people had escaped to Skyberia to avoid annihilation."

"And?"

"He found them, and to save anymore loss of lives, our people gave themselves up to him- willingly. Most of the young people were made to destroy cities on other planets with his armies. The rest were put to work in the Gorin factories building their new warships. They have been treated poorly. If they have not all died by now, they are better off that way," Tresodin, heavy hearted, stared at the floor as he let himself out.

"What are you going to do, Kamarin?"

"Didn't you hear him? There isn't anything anyone can do for them now."

"But Kamarin, what if they use our own people against us in battle?"

"Then it will be Voltar's last mistake!"

"Thirteen"

Having won their first conflict, Kamarin gathered his people together into the underground city center encircling the river conduit feeding its fountain.

Erin, Lort, Tresodin, and Decker all stood in front of the crowd intent on hearing what Kamarin had to say. This would be the last time they would all meet before the battle begins.

The Thelonans quietly visited among themselves while they waited for their Guardian.

Then like a wave, they stopped all discussion as he stepped up before them.

"My precious brothers and sisters of wonderful Thelona! How proud I am of you all. You have worked hard and must be commended, but now our preparation must take yet another turn, for tomorrow we must separate our defenses into 'two' forces."

The crowd began to mumble to each other in some attempt to avoid questioning his decision.

"I realize that we all feel we are safer as a large group, but if the Gorin are allowed to attack us now and win, then goes the battle! We cannot afford to be in our present position. So, I have decided, most of our air command will stay here in this city, with Tresodin as their commander. The rest of us will disburse into other areas of Thelona. This will make it difficult for Voltar and his men to locate us and allow us to strike first without warning. Unfortunately there can be no other way. So tonight, return to your quarters and gather up your possessions, for tomorrow we depart!" Kamarin paused as if waiting for arguments, but his people trusted him implicitly and would comply without fail.

When Kamarin did leave his people, they all turned to one another and hugged each other realizing that the time had come. They were afraid that this might be their last good-byes. The end of Thelona could be at hand.

The Thelonan's fear soon took its rightful place, and they started sorting through their personals, and their weaponry for the move.

After the meeting Lort, Decker, and Tresodin, waited patiently for Erin and Kamarin to join them at one of the garden room tables for a farewell feast. But since the two of them were obviously late, Tresodin excused himself to find and bring them to dinner.

Having a hunch Kamarin might be in his quarters, the old scientist tried there first.

Suddenly he heard what sounded like an argument between the two of them.

Hesitant at first, but curious, he waited outside before knocking to enter. Eavesdropping, he listened to what was being said.

"Kamarin, don't you realize there is absolutely nothing you can do right now?" Erin said, undoubtedly frustrated.

"Why, Erin? I'm supposed to be their Guardian, remember? Those people are counting on me, too."

"Those people have no idea that you even exist, Kamarin."

"Still, I must do something to help them. I just can't imagine those people having to bow to the Gorin taskmasters all of these years."

With that Tresodin knew what was troubling Kamarin and decided to knock and knocked loudly.

"Come in!" Erin said, briefly interrupting her conversation.

"Kamarin, I couldn't help listening to you two. I beg your pardon but you must realize this is wrong."

"What is wrong, Tresodin?" asked Kamarin.

"Those people were taken from this planet twenty years ago, Guardian. They could not be alive today."

"How can you be so sure of that, Tresodin, you're still here."

"Well, I have no proof except that the Gorin are terribly vengeful and the likelihood that they may have survived is very doubtful."

"If it were you or I, wouldn't you want to be rescued?" asked Kamarin.

"You forget who you are talking about, Guardian, they are Thelonans. They are the most resourceful in the galaxy."

"Besides Kamarin, we need you here, all of you. Not just part of you. The war is here, and now," Erin said, squeezing his shoulders, trying to bring him back to reality.

"Then there will be another time," he said, as he finally became calm and again aware of the matter at hand.

"Let's go get something to eat, OK?" Erin asked, taking them both by the arm, leading them out of the room.

The next morning brought some confusion as to where his people were being sent. Some family members were accidentally split-up. This definitely was not what Kamarin ordered, the situation was quickly corrected and the boarding of his people to their respective vehicles was continued.

The word was finally given and the multitude proceeded up the ramp of the underground air station. Some of the ground machines climbed the long steel grate while others flew to the above freedom. In all that were to leave they numbered over thirty-five thousand. Of the group, twenty thousand were to follow Decker to the south.

Kamarin, Erin, and Lort were now inseparable and left together. Their ship was a combination Land Runner and a Sky Rover. The rover held in its belly a Thelonan Land Runner that could detach when the need arose. The Sky Rover was filled with advanced surveillance equipment, it held very little in armament. The Rover's speed ranged from a gargantuan Buckarian Butterfly to that of over time speed. The time speed however, was a trade off of not having 'hovering' capabilities. This was acceptable to

Kamarin, though because he could not see hanging around when there was too much trouble anyway.

Also accompanying the three of them, were three of Kamarin's metal men. His mother's two and the dead Guardian's. The fourth was left behind with Tresodin, because of its special flying capabilities.

It was not important for Kamarin to be with him to give him orders. It seemed to know what it was that it was required for it to do. Another strange attribute of his metal men was that they appeared to communicate between themselves. How was this possible? Only the creator knew of their power.

Their destination was the city that Kamarin had found during his reconnaissance flight. He knew nothing about it, but his plan was to set up a defensive force just outside the city's perimeter. This would allow his people quick access to the nearby forest to take refuge in when the Gorin invaded.

Between the city and the forest was a small, rocky, mountain range. Kamarin planned to use the rock formations as a lookout station as the first line of defense. The city itself however, would be off limits. It would not serve well as a battlefield.

Tresodin had indicated that yet another large city was almost as far, but in the opposite direction, to the south. That is where Kamarin decided to send Decker and the women and children.

From the Sky Rover, Decker's group could be seen veering off to the right of his group and down into the horizon. Kamarin prayed that he had made the right decision and that the Gorin would not attack there first. He hoped that they would not have to see much of the fighting about to erupt on Thelona.

The city of their destination was already in sight in the far distance. It was so large that it looked very close but actually was quite far away and was going to take them at least two days to reach it.

Kamarin felt strongly about not engaging the Gorin inside its gates because it would almost mean certain death for the Thelonanas. Still, his curiosity of exploring where his people had once lived was quite enticing.

It was awesome, and he could not keep his eyes from it. Was it possible for someone to have been left behind there? Or was it truly a city of the 'lost' as Tresodin had described it to be?

Flying over his people in their ground machines, Kamarin guided them to their new destination. It really was not necessary for him to do so but they expected to see him from time to time for the encouragement.

The young adults rode atop their parents' treaders and waved constantly to the Guardian. In response to them he would wave the wing tips of the Sky Rover just to see them smile and wave all the more.

Among the treader machines were their newly created war machines, such as the two seated Prowler. A hydraulically driven, six legged, assault vehicle. Very fast, very effective and very new. In fact, the Gorin had yet to get a taste of their highly advanced machines especially this one.

Then there was the Buster, a speeder treader with a laser turret and having only forward motion. One soldier operated it. He would literally drive into the enemy line while the lasers above his head fired wildly. The Buster would leave a path of devastation and weaken the enemy's defenses. After busting its way through the first time, it would then make a large circle and start over again. Their machines were simple but they made good use of surprise.

The third morning of their travels brought them all just a few hours away from the city.

Assembled again they were back on the road. Everyone was enjoying the trip taking in the freshness of Thelona's air and filling their eyes with its beauty.

Kamarin had hitched a ride with the lead vehicle just to be closer to his people.

One of the older children yelled to his friends who were riding on the other treader machines.

"Hey, let's play Gorin spy!"

Kamarin immediately realized that the children had just made up their new game. As he watched, he could only hope that their simulated deaths would not become a reality. He vowed to himself, that one-day the children would not have to worry about war. After all children need to be children, and war, is far from child's play.

"Fourteen"

Before they reached the city, Kamarin stopped his people in the forest adjacent to the rocky cliffs separating them from it.

It was here that they would build their base camps. Strategically he planned to locate his marksmen throughout the rock formations. When this was completed, Kamarin planned to visit the city to explore some of his other options.

With the main assault on Thelona expected now at any time, time was a gift that was not being wasted.

Using the maze of trails through the undergrowth on the forest floor, a shelter was made for each warrior and was interconnected by small tunnels in the flora.

Having been exiled from Thelona for the long period they were a tolerant people. Kamarin's people had become well adapt' to these kinds of living conditions. They knew that with the arrival of the

Gorin, came the almost certain destruction of their cities. So it was here they would stay and fight.

With the new settlement completed, the Guardian and his friends led the Thelonan warriors to the natural rocky parapets.

Three lookout stations were established and between them more than five thousand warriors.

Now everyone quietly and patiently waited for the most important battle in 'all' of the Orion galaxy.

It wasn't cold that night but Erin still shivered nervously as Kamarin held her. Although the mood was light, tensions were high and Erin was unintentionally elevating her own anxiety.

They both stood together watching the sunset behind the massive buildings of the city, casting ghostly shadows in the valley.

Kamarin reflected back on his life leading up to this moment. With very little success, he tried to contemplate where his parents might have gone, in their after-life.

He remembered his mother's loving and guiding hand and how his father raised him to be a strong, but yet a compassionate man. Kamarin worked very hard trying to emulate their love. Outside forces often had a negative influence on him but he honored his parents too much to let things sway him. Now he was about to confront an old and new enemy and he could not ask for a better hand to play. The advantage was now his. And he would not give in, until Voltar and his friend Ogel, were stopped once and for all.

Another beautiful night on Thelona and the sea of stars and planets above seemed so close they could just float from one planet to the other.

227

Most everyone could not sleep this night and planet gazing seemed to be the entertainment of the evening.

A few hours into the night, Kamarin and Erin snuggled each other to sleep, cradled between a few large rocks, lending themselves as a wind-break.

Then Lort suddenly spotted approaching lights that definitely were not falling stars. He quickly made his way to his two friends.

"Guardian! They're coming!" Lort said in a loud whisper, nudging Kamarin's shoulder trying not to wake Erin. But Kamarin jumped up, startling her.

"Where are they?" she asked.

"There-see!" Lort said pointing.

By this time, there was a steady onslaught of lights that could be seen entering the Thelonan atmosphere in many different locations.

Many of them were coming at meteorite speeds, except some of the much larger ones. Of those, Kamarin counted at least nine. He knew what kind of ships they were and could only hope there would be no more.

Kamarin turned quickly to Erin and grabbed her by her arms, lifting her to her feet, the ones that were now a very much part of her. Then she smiled. Except he could not see what was so humorous and looked at her questioningly.

"My foot's asleep," she said, still grinning from ear to ear.

He too then smiled and took her with one hand behind her head, giving her a big kiss, looking down at her legs.

Lort could not contain himself any longer. "You kids look sweet together, but don't you think you should put that on hold? At least until this is over?"

"You know how it is, don't you, big guy?" Kamarin said, giving Lort a wink as he picked up his pack.

Erin just smiled.

"No, I do not know how it 'is'. My race never did any of that."

"Well, I'm shocked, large one. Just what is it you did do?" Kamarin asked, ribbing him.

"That, my dear friend, is none of your business."

"Sorry, Lort, but what I have to tell you now, is," Kamarin said, becoming totally serious for a moment. "My friends…we have to go into the city."

"No, Kamarin, that would be suicide," said Erin.

"Not all of us, Erin, just a small group. We have to lure them into the city. Then we can cut off their escape routes and contain the battle there. It took our ancestors decades to build Thelona into the wondrous place it is now. And if they intend to destroy our cities, then let it be this one only. I will sacrifice no other to them."

"But what if they attack Decker's city first?" Erin asked.

"Don't ask me how, but I just know that they will look for me here. That is why I sent Decker to the other."

Kamarin loathed fortune-tellers and would never claim to be one, but his dreams were now leading his heart. Everyone in the next life, especially his parents who had appeared to him as angels of war, were apparently guiding his steps now.

"OK, Kamarin, I'm with you. Wherever you want to go I'll go. No, 'we' will go," Erin said, pulling Lort closer.

"When do we attack, Guardian?" asked Lort.

"No time like the present. Lort, get me three of the elite guards to travel with us."

"That is all? Never mind," Lort said and then lumbered off.

"It doesn't look like we will get much rest tonight, Erin." Kamarin said as if he were asking her if she had any objections.

"I couldn't sleep now even if I were knocked unconscious," she said.

Erin followed Kamarin down a long sloping trail, towards the city.

Close behind was Lort and three highly trained Thelonan soldiers.

It would take them all of half the night just to reach the city's limits.

The streets were very dark, and the stars became the only source of light; casting an eerie blue haze on everything exposed.

To the reconnaissance team- it became all too apparent that there was no way to differentiate live objects from inanimate ones. Everything seemed to move at a glance.

Uncomfortable with the situation, Kamarin detached the metal man from his wristband and sent it off down one of the darkened streets. Flying around as though it were some kind of pixy, it glowed brightly, illuminating the way. And the way was clear.

Well into the city they stopped to reconnoiter the area. The metal man swooped in and out of the surrounding abandoned buildings to assure their safety. Then he returned to Kamarin and stood guard. His light dimmed so as not to give away their position.

Deke's light faintly grew to let Kamarin know he, too was ready in case he was needed.

The next morning found the group asleep in the street wherever they could make themselves comfortable.

But when Erin woke and found Lort and Kamarin gone, she snapped into a nervous consciousness. Rousting the others, she commanded them to follow her.

Rounding one of the corners, at the base of a mammoth building reaching into the sky, she was almost run over by Lort as he breezed by her.

"What's going on?" she asked.

"Get back! Get back!" Lort yelled waving at her.

Right behind him was Kamarin, his eyes wide.

"Get back! Get back!" Kamarin repeated Lort's warning.

"Why? Why?" Erin asked, as she started to run with them.

"That's why!" Kamarin said, pointing up above the street lamp jutting out from the building's third story. Hovering quietly towards them was a Gorin Drone ship, only a couple of feet in diameter, doing much the same thing his metal man had done the night before.

"I think it spotted us," said Lort when the Drone sped past and then shot straight up.

"Mmm, then again maybe it didn't." said Kamarin.

"Then again, maybe it did," Erin said after turning around to check behind them. There it was again, motionless; staying high above the ground after it had discovered them.

Everyone just suddenly opened fire on it trying to shoot it down. But their laser blasts had no affect on it. Kamarin's metal man grew from out of nowhere in a flash, to the same height as the Gorin Drone.

As if he were swatting a fly from the air, he raised his hands, clapping them together down on the probe ship. The thing, or what was left of it, simply fell to the ground with a shower of sparks.

The metal man cocked his head from one side to the other watching the different colors fall from his hands.

"Well, it's a cinch they know we're here now," Lort said, shaking his head.

"Yes and I could not have sent a better invitation myself," Kamarin said grinning slyly.

The metal man had reduced in size again. This time, to about as big as a human fist. He constantly traveled ahead from then on, floating ankle high and still darting in and out of buildings securing their path along the way.

Farther and farther, Kamarin and his companions ventured into the city, always on guard now for another unexpected visitor.

Erin could almost swear that she was hearing the humming of Gorin fighter ships from above but none were cited.

When they came to that part of the city where all the streets converged, the team noticed a strange cloud had quickly formed and enveloped the tops of the buildings above. They observed it slowly descending down to them. Everyone seemed on edge as it came closer.

Then suddenly it became clear as to what it was, when here there and everywhere, Gorin attack fighters swooped down surrounding them. The cloud was a trick, a clever smoke screen.

With their weapons raised, Kamarin motioned to the others 'not' to shoot for he knew if they did it would be for the last time. They were surrounded.

Standing at bay, he began to wonder why the ship keeping them from escaping, did not fire on them. Stepping forward, Kamarin calls to its occupant.

"Well! What are you waiting for? You obviously have us at a great disadvantage! Tell me who is leading this attack?"

As the hatch opened at the top of the ship, a familiar face appeared. Kamarin's old acquaintance, Ogel!

"It's been a long time, hasn't it, my friend?" he said.

"Oh, how different it might have been if you really were a friend," said Kamarin smiling, folding his arms relaxed in a non-threatening attitude.

"Tell me truly, Kamarin. Who would want to be my friend?"

"Cut to the chase, Ogel! You know why we are here and it is not to have any sort of play on words. And where is your master? Shouldn't he be sitting where you are?"

"No! He is an old man. Besides, when he finds out that I alone have finished what he had set out to do, he might want to pin a medal on me."

233

"Somehow I figured you to have more intelligence than that, Ogel. He has just been using you. Can't you see that?"

"And I let him! Trust me Kamarin, I know what I'm doing."

"Oh, you do, Hugh?"

"Yes. And absolutely none of my people doubt me." Ogel stood tall in his open cockpit of the hovering Gorin fighter.

"Is that right? Well, none of my warriors doubt me either, in fact, here, let me introduce you to one." Kamarin quickly detached Deke from his headband and threw him under Ogel's fighter.

Instantly, Deke grew to meet Ogel eye to eye and took the ship by its short wings, and began to tear them off. Ogel held on for his dear- life trying with all his might not to fall out of his seat and out of his fighter.

Kamarin could see that Ogel's eyes were now big and white with fear. Kamarin's metal man succeeded in causing the wingless fuselage to crash to the ground with its horrified cargo. The whole incident took just a matter of seconds after which the other ships started their barrage on the Thelonans. But before they could hit their targets, Kamarin's other metal man had also taken on a larger shape and was attacking them wildly for the air.

He quickly grabbed them spinning each one around until they, in all their confusion, blasted each other and they simply blew-up!

Kamarin had taken his eyes off Ogel for a minute too long. For when he checked the wreckage of his ship, he was nowhere to be found. And unfortunately his friends did not see him escape either. He was a very lucky character but 'his time' in the 'sun' was over- a long time ago.

Kamarin, Erin, and two of his elite warriors continued searching for Ogel after having sent Lort back to gather reinforcements.

Kamarin's metal men stood by guarding the street while they searched the ground level of the building closest to the wreck. It was entirely possible that he may have taken refuge in the giant building.

Still there was no sight of him or any other Gorin survivors.

Not having found a body and believing he had somehow escaped, Kamarin decided he, for the moment, posed no immediate threat. So, he motioned to his small group to exit the building.

"Erin?"

"Yes, Kamarin?"

"I want you to check on our people in the forest. Would you?" Kamarin asked as if begging to try and protect her.

"Kamarin," she said, shaking her head no. "I know what you're doing and its not going to work. Just because things got out of hand a little doesn't mean I'm going to go hide somewhere. I told you that I plan to stay with you no matter what. And if you think I'm quitting after we've just started, you would have a better chance giving my pet cat a hug."

Kamarin looked at Erin with the understanding that with one more word, he could be facing a confrontation he definitely would rather avoid. So, with his head bowed, he tried making a hasty retreat.

"Take cover! Don't go any further, they're coming!" Erin said suddenly, waving and pointing to the horizon at the other end of the city.

Just as Kamarin waved for his warriors to take cover, the first Gorin assault came with three of their fighters on a strafing run. Kamarin was a bit startled, not having seen them coming with his back turned.

Large laser blasts exploded around him as he jumped for cover.

When he looked to check on Erin, he saw that she was safe, but she had gone to the opposite side of the street. He motioned for her to stay down. Then he watched as more fighters came down.

The prowler drivers were very quick this time, and had driven their six-legged war machines right up the sides of the buildings. Kamarin was happy to see that the Gorin 'only' managed to split up their formation with their first pass. As their sharp feet dug into the concrete, the prowlers stayed attached to the monoliths, the same way a spider would.

Then at least eight more fighters followed through with yet another run.

Except this time his warriors were poised and caught them in a cross-fire easily blasting them from the sky.

It was quiet now but for how long? One of the prowlers backed its way down from its perch on the side of a building made of marble rock.

Erin could see that it was Lort through the dark canopy.

He had been riding shotgun in it!

"Guardian!" Lort yelled when the top popped open. "We have word from the sixth and ninth group that most of our other prowlers are engaged in battle, with many Gorin fighters outside the city…Wait!"

"How are they faring, Lort?" asked Kamarin.

Lort listened to the rest of the message coming in on his headset.

"Well…At first not too well, but they have just been joined by five hundred Thelonan air fighters Tresodin has sent!" he said with a smile.

Kamarin immediately felt more comfortable. "Then it is there that we must join the fight." He turned to his fighters then ordered all of them to rejoin the main body of fighters on the plains outside the city to fight the war that would end all others.

Having left the confines of the city for the hilly plains, where his people were in full involvement with the Gorin, they could see that many of the enemy- had fallen.

Kamarin, alone with Erin, stood on a slightly higher hill than the rest to enable him to assess the situation at hand.

He watched as several enemy fighters took turns trying to attack his men who were driving the prowlers. Not one of them sustained any real damage from their laser blasts. All that the enemy could really do was temporarily separate them- only to have them quickly regroup.

Very soon it was again night. All that was revealed to him, as to the location of his people, were the driving lights of the prowlers and the occasional explosion of enemy fighters. The sky would light up as they fell from it, or blew up into it.

With all of the fighting that was taking place, there had been no sign of their leader, or of the enemy's new weapon, the giant 'holographs'.

Separate from the close proximity of the all-out battle taking place, Kamarin could see one of his metal men at work over near the rocky cliffs where his people were assembled.

He was busily destroying any and all Gorin fighters that dared to get too close to them.

On the other hand Deke was nowhere to be found. And he certainly was too big now 'not' to have been sighted. Kamarin had seen one of the large warships destroyed off in the distance. It did appear to have been Deke's handiwork. It was also unusual to not have any Gorin foot soldiers to contend with.

Kamarin could not shake the eery feeling that something was terribly wrong. No other explanation could be given except that the Gorin were up to something, but what? Where was Deke?

The noise of the battle started to fade and it seemed to bring Kamarin out of his dream-state and back to reality. The Gorin fighters had stopped coming and his people now, were quietly waiting for the next wave.

But it was not to come.

The huge Gorin battleships that were on the horizon were slowly encroaching upon the now heavily defended territory, and Curiously without any fighter escort. Kamarin called for a cease-fire.

He believed that the time for conversation was over, but he also was one for allowing mercy, and one couldn't offer mercy 'without' conversation. It was possible that they planned to surrender to him, but he knew that the Gorin, specifically Voltar, could not be trusted and that the game he was playing would not be over as easily as this.

So while he and his friends stood together patiently waiting for the enemy's ships to come into range, the stand-down order not to fire, was being adhered to.

They stood ready now for anything.

Three of the Gorin battleships stopped just outside range, while a lone ship proceeded into the war zone.

With every trained gun alert the enemy ship slowly approached, and then came to a stop.

The battle cruiser was an impressive sight. Its ominous splendor was indeed representative of its Gorin leader's vanity. But even with the outstanding hews of color gleaming from its shining surface, it could not extinguish the light from the piles of their burning fighters reflecting off its surface.

Kamarin was more disgusted and not very impressed.

In a flash an elevator shaft was plunged to the ground with its occupant, Voltar.

"We meet again, Kamarin Mitchel," Voltar said, staying well away and close to the protection of his ship.

"Yes and for the last time. Oh- take him!" Kamarin motioned for his people to arrest Voltar. But Voltar raised his hand.

"I would think twice if I were you, my old friend," he said, stepping back as two menacing holographic figures appeared on each side of him, standing about twenty feet tall.

The Thelonans were on guard and ready, but the figures were not moving yet.

Interested, but still not amused, Kamarin's confidence slipped a 'bit' as his metal men did not come immediately to their aid to combat the sudden intruders.

Where are they? He thought, nonchalantly looking around for at least a sign from them. For some reason, they seemed to have disappeared.

Their standoff suddenly became one-sided.

"Are you looking for these?" Voltar asked laughing as he held up two metal objects. "Since the 'great' war I have invented many things. Standing before you are just a sample. I have also had enough time to discover a way of making your metal men useless!"

Kamarin stood in shock, as did his friends.

"You no longer pose any threat to me, Kamarin. Now, who is going to submit to the other?" Voltar defiantly threw the metal figures to the ground.

All of Kamarin's people were beginning to lower their weapons in surrender.

Then from off in the distance behind them, the plains of Thelona began to erupt with the sounds of war again.

It was Decker! And the rest of Kamarin's people, escorted by the elite air command led by Tresodin, and in the middle of it all were the other two metal men of Thelona.

Then suddenly that familiar glow came from the two figures at Voltar's feet. Answering a call to justice, in a flash of an eye, the metal men grew to face and attack their opponents- the Gorin holographs.

During the confusion, Voltar managed to escape back to the protection of the battle cruiser.

The fighting quickly spread to their location and there could be no mistake that now was the time of the "independence of Orion."

As Kamarin swung his long sword between throwing ribstingers, Erin stuck with him protecting his blind side.

It soon became apparent to Kamarin that his people had now been joined by almost every race of beings in the galaxy.

"What? How in the…? How did you get here? I thought you were dead!" Kamarin yelled to an old friend. It was Bugboody!

"Did you see me die, Guardian?" he asked Kamarin as they both continued fighting.

"Well, no, but…"

"Don't feel that bad, they never saw us when we built the bridges either!"

Kamarin was elated, his smile could be seen by many and the feeling spread to his people like a firestorm.

They fought fearsomely into the dawn.

Kamarin and his friends were starting to test the great fatigue of it all.

From the corner of his eye, he noticed bodies were falling everywhere.

But when he looked to see what was taking place, he saw his mother and his father standing back to back, fighting much the same way as he and Erin were.

They were laying waste to yet another strange sort of being. It was apparent that Kamarin alone was able to see this similar battle taking place in a different world beyond their own.

Robin L. Amrine

With a wave, one, then the other, acknowledged Kamarin. Then his parents faded away into what must have been their own 'new-world' somewhere, in possibly another time.

As the greatest of Thelona's battles came to a close, they all began to assess the damage it had caused.

Gorin bodies were everywhere but there was no sign of Voltar or Ogel. With all of the destruction, how could they have escaped again?

Frustrated beyond belief, Kamarin went on the hunt. He was looking for anything that might give him a clue as to where they might have gone.

His people were busy pulling the dead from the huge warships. Some of which were badly charred still, no sign of his rival enemies.

"Kamarin!" Erin solemnly asked for his attention.

"What?" he asked.

"I was just talking to Decker and he said that he and Lort just watched a crippled fighter fly into a small canyon not far from here. He said he saw Lort trying follow it."

"VOLTAR!" Kamarin perked up quickly with the welcome news. "Where is this canyon?"

"Decker said it was over in that direction!" Erin waved her long knife towards some rocky cliffs near the city. "He said it emptied out there."

"Where did he see him go in?" Kamarin asked as they made their way to it.

"Right over there!" she turned and pointed in the opposite direction.

"Why didn't you say so?" he asked her.

"You did not ask."

With no further waste of time, Kamarin took off running with Erin in hot pursuit.

It was not long and they came upon a rather small canyon that looked as if it zigzagged around one side of the rocky-mountains and emptied before the city.

"Why wasn't I told this was here? This must have been how Ogel escaped from us after attacking us in the city."

"I didn't know it was here," Erin said, shrugging her shoulders.

Both of them walked along its edge, peering down into the crevasses periodically.

Then Kamarin spotted something he feared most.

Lying at the bottom of the gorge was one of the metal men he had been searching for. Motionless, there was no mistaking that the giants power supply or whatever it was, had completely drained from him.

Even though all of Voltar's evil warships had been destroyed, by his metal men the task had proven to be too great. Kamarin had not yet been able to locate the other but he was afraid it might have met the same sort of fate.

In a kind of reverent gesture, he took his headband from his head and bowed to the giant. He was thankful that both of his other metal men had reappeared to their original size and were safely attached again where they belonged.

"Thank you friend for your help," Kamarin said addressing his fallen metal giant, and putting his shiny band back on his head he continued on.

As Erin passed, she paused as if she too wanted to say something but turned quickening her pace to catch up with Kamarin and fell in rhythm by his side.

A short distance away they could hear an intermittent whirring sound.

There could be no mistaking it. It was a Gorin fighter.

Their paces quickened as they approached the canyon again and looked over the edge.

This time it was pay-day! Slowly turning, hovering and glancing off the gorge walls was the enemy fighter. It had taken a hit, and it was too damaged now, to be safely controlled.

However, the Gorin pilot was stubborn and had not abandoned it.

Kamarin stood to address its driver.

"I am Kamarin! Kamarin Mitchel, Guardian of this planet! Driver, give it up before the machine takes you with it! Let yourself be recognized and you will be treated fairly!"

When the hatch flew open, Kamarin was surprised to see its occupant.

The fighter stopped its lazy spin long enough for Ogel to pop up from the cockpit.

"We've got to stop meeting like this, Kamarin," Ogel said, quickly sitting back down to momentarily regain control of the listing aircraft.

"It certainly hasn't been a very good day for you, has it Ogel?" Kamarin replied.

"Tell me, Kamarin, Guardian of Thelona, how exactly would you know?" Ogel said, quickly sitting down and then popped up again.

"Ogel- give up this nonsense and come back with us. You needn't go on with this masquerade." Kamarin tried to appeal to Ogel's better half. Unfortunately for him, he didn't know he had one.

"Kamarin, my old friend, you just don't get it, do you? What do you think you've gained?"

The fighter craft was becoming even 'more unstable, now small electrical fires began to burn and smoke finding its way out and around Ogel.

"Come on, Ogel! Listen to Kamarin, he's just trying to help you! Or are you really that blind?" Erin yelled to him.

"Ogel! Your fighter is going to blow up and if you don't get out now you won't have a chance! Ogel, Voltar was just using you, you know this! Ogel, listen to me!" Kamarin held out his hand.

"Your right, Kamarin. You couldn't be more right! He used me right to the end you know? I even helped him to escape, and you were too blind to see us." Ogel said, laughing and fidgeting with the controls again, struggling terribly to breath through the smoke.

Kamarin quickly became alarmed. "What are you saying, Ogel?"

"I'm saying that the old man got the hell out of here, and left me to burn!" Ogel started to laugh again, only nervously this time.

Suddenly an explosion blasted a hole out of the back of the craft.

"Ugh-Oh!" he said, sitting down again for the last time as the ship spun wildly loosing altitude.

"See you in the next life, Kamarin old friend! I am sorry!" were Ogel's last words as his fighter sped up, smashing into the far wall of the small gorge, exploding into small burning chunks of metal.

"You have lost in this life, Ogel, but maybe you will have a better chance in the next one, if you indeed make it there- old friend." Kamarin said, turning his attention to the sky in hopes that he might someday see him again, and make the wrongs right for a change.

Kamarin, and Erin, walked slowly away from Ogel's burning ship after briefly inspecting the area for a hopeless chance of a survivor, but the fragments that were left were hardly making note of. There would be no one surviving this crash.

Even though Kamarin wasn't the least bit responsible for Ogel's actions, his needless loss of life disturbed him.

-*-

Now- the renewed faith for the future brought many neighboring beings to Thelona. All who had come were there to see the new Guardian. He would eventually meet those who were coming to welcome him, but there was a little matter he had to attend to first.

As he finished dressing himself in a very fine suit of clothes Bugboody's wife made for him, Erin let herself in unannounced. She too was dressed to impress. Although their cloths were not expensive, they were presentable.

"Are you ready, Kamarin?"

"Yes," he said, presenting his elbow for her.

Standing outside in the hall was Lort and, of course, Decker. They too were dressed for the part. They were there to escort Kamarin and Erin to one of the biggest celebrations the Orion galaxy had seen in a very long time.

Decker bowed down on one knee before Kamarin.

"We would be honored to be your escorts Guardian, if you would allow us," Decker said.

"Of course you can," said Erin, "but we have something to do first."

"But, little lady, I…" Lort tried to interject.

"With your patience, of course, Lort," she added.

"Lead on, little one," Lort said in a gruff voice.

They followed as Kamarin lead them to another building in the great city, by way of an underground transit car.

He had brought them to the prisoner holding area where some of the survivors of the war were being kept.

His eyes met with Kotch's from down the long hall.

"Am I to be made a spectacle at your party?" Kotch yelled, trying to be defiant unto the end. Even as afraid as he was for his life.

Kamarin stood at the doorway that was blocked by large shards of glass to keep in the prisoners.

"Kotch- Ogel was killed during the fight," Kamarin reluctantly told him.

Kotch just stared at Kamarin for a moment; his eyes filled with tears and he then collapsed to the floor.

"Kotch. If you wish to have another chance, we are willing to accept you and the others as citizens of Thelona. But if it is your wish that you die as a sort of martyr, then so be- it, and we will leave."

"Please, Kamarin," Kotch looked up at him, "I want life!" he said. "I want to 'live', I will change!"

"Good! Very good then, let- them go," Kamarin ordered an attending guard.

"Guardian! Oh- no, Your not serious?" said Decker with a look of surprise.

"He has no reason to be against us anymore," Kamarin said and opened the door himself.

Kotch fell at his feet crying almost hysterically.

"But Guardian, he is our enemy," said Lort.

"All of our enemies are now dead! And only the living remain." Kamarin turned to Erin again giving her his arm for her to walk with him to the festivities, and they walked away.

"Is he sure he wants to do this?" Decker asked Lort.

"If he orders this done, then that is what will be. He is the Guardian."

The armies of the galaxy gathered on the plains outside of the great city to give tribute to Kamarin and his friends.

Kamarin turned to Erin- "Has anyone reported back about Voltar?" His voice was elevated over the crowds.

"No Kamarin, no one has found him."

"It would have calmed my spirit more if someone had."

"But Kamarin- its over, we've won!" she smiled and hugged him.

Kamarin had a fearful feeling something had been left undone. It was a feeling he was sure would haunt him.

Stepping out onto a balcony high above the crowd in the 'mega city', the roar of the people's appreciation was awesome.

Kamarin's metal men joined them- stepping around each corner of the skyscraper. They stood tall, as they took up their positions on each side of the Guardian and his friends on the balcony, high above his people.

The applause grew…

And it was good!

Thelona… was free…

About the Author

Robin L. Amrine is an Artist and a singer-songwriter since the young age of eight. With his wife of 25 years, three daughters and a grandchild, he has finally realized the novelist in him.

The stories in his songs and his pictures he's painted, were just hints of his true creativity. His 'true' release comes from the written word.

Believing that good does triumph over evil, he has always wanted to give people hope. There is more to this world than hate.

When he found his daughters were reading nightmarish stories, he decided they- and even some adults, needed to know- there is a good side to all we see. Thus he created—"Mom's Metal Men."

Printed in the United States
1432600001B/232-237